WAITING FOR LUIGI

WAITING FOR LUIGI

SOMETIMES THE PAST IS BEST LEFT BURIED...
OR IS IT?

SANDRA DUCLOS, Ph.D.

AUTHOR ACADEMY elite

Printed in the United States of America

Published by Author Academy Elite
PO Box 43, Powell, OH 43035
www.AuthorAcademyElite.com

Identifiers:
LCCN: 2019908867
ISBN: 978-1-64085-755-1 (paperback)
ISBN: 978-1-64085-756-8 (hardback)
ISBN: 978-1-64085-757-5 (E-book)

Available in paperback, hardback, e-book, and audiobook.

Book design by Chris O'Byrne of JetLaunch.
Cover Design by rados777@99designs.com/profiles/878698

For Duke, Jason, Chrystal, JJ, and Ryan with profound love.
They are my family, my greatest blessings, my joy, my heart,
and my life.

CONTENTS

ACKNOWLEDGMENTS

Many people have contributed to this book in countless ways, and I wish to acknowledge them here.

Ferman Duclos: First and foremost, I am grateful to my husband, "Duke." Your faith in me, encouragement, support, and generous heart sustained me. You made this book possible, and I am so blessed to have you as my life partner.

Deb Montanaro: My niece has been an angel sitting on my shoulder from the beginning. Your belief in my ability, encouragement, honest feedback, and insights were priceless, and I am indebted to you.

Linda and Michael Poole: I am so grateful for your helpful comments, encouragement, and cherished friendship.

Danielle Rymer: Your insightful and respectful editing made for a better end-product and is much appreciated.

Kary Oberbrunner and his entire staff at Author Academy Elite: You are publishers extraordinaire. You held my hand throughout the process, providing expert advice, kindness, warmth, and an unwavering belief in my book. You were so responsive to my endless questions and made my dream a reality.

Thank you all.

"Be strong and courageous. Do not fear or be in dread of them, for it is the LORD your God who goes with you. He will not leave you or forsake you."

Deuteronomy 31:6
The Holy Bible
English Standard Version

"The mind is its own place, and in itself can make a hell of heaven, a heaven of hell."

John Milton
Paradise Lost
(1667)

1

THE DECISION

The self-doubt creeps back in as if it had never left. *Could this be a big mistake? Is it worth the risk?* Angela weighs her options again but continues to waver in her decision. The mere thought of it causes her stomach to churn. She trembles as she seeks reassurance from her husband, hoping he will tell her she is making a mistake. But he cannot answer his wife's questions, calm her fears, or decide for her. He promises though, to stand by her even if Angela's greatest fears materialize: the nightmares and flashbacks return, and her decision ruins her happiness.

Although she has faced and conquered many daunting challenges, this one makes her think she is weak. So much is at stake. Despite her fear-driven wavering and procrastination, and regardless of what she wants to do, Angela Carcieri Limoges knows what she must do. After squelching the nausea that arose with her decision, she heads to the airport, prepping herself for battle.

Yes, it's a risk, but I will never be free unless I take it. No more delays. Now is the time. Lord, please help me!

Angela retired from her successful, Manhattan-based law firm ten months ago. As an attorney who specialized in custody cases, she dedicated herself to fighting for the best interests of the minors involved. The wealth and prestige she gained from

1

her work were not her priority. What mattered most to Angela was protecting those children. She devoted herself to each case and represented only those parents who best nurtured their offspring. As a result, Angela won the overwhelming majority of her lawsuits and built a sterling reputation.

Often, the cases she handled had been heartbreaking. When the inept parents she opposed loved their children, watching them lose custody was difficult. Sometimes, Angela thought she was playing God and had no business doing so. She managed the guilt by reminding herself that the child's welfare trumped everything else. Although Angela sympathized with the parents, her heart was always with the children. She now misses the challenge and satisfaction she got from her work, but, although she retired, she still has one last little girl to fight for and free: the wounded child within herself.

Her flight lands in the early morning, and she releases a sigh of relief as she unfolds her tall, slender body from the cramped airplane seat. Angela heads to the nearest restroom in the terminal to examine her still-smooth face, making sure she is presentable after the long flight. God forbid a single hair is out of place, or her grooming looks less than impeccable.

At least my insomnia hasn't caused those ugly under-eye circles.

She straightens the jacket of her expensive, black outfit. Black clothing befits her mood; Angela, who has been reflecting on her life since retirement, is mourning the loss of her youth, the end of her career, and her stolen childhood.

Before picking up her rental car, she grabs a cup of strong tea at an airport concession for the caffeine she needs to fuel her journey. Not bothering to stop at the hotel first, Angela clenches the steering wheel with white knuckles for the fifteen-minute drive to Rockport, the small New England town where she spent her early childhood. The beach is her first stop.

As she stands at the shore, to acclimate and calm herself, Angela studies the swells in the sea and the ebb and flow of the tide against the fine-grained, beige sand glistening in the sun. The October air makes her pull her jacket tighter and button her collar against the breezes rolling off the water. A lone jogger and her handsome golden retriever are the only others occupying the beach, so Angela has the privacy she needs. She smiles as she watches the pair jog along the shoreline, passing a rugged man and a young boy fishing from the dock. The dog looks so content being with his mistress. He barks while the wind ruffles his fur and he runs to keep pace with her.

While watching the dog, Angela remembers her old sidekick, Fluffy. He had been the neighbor's pet she played with on this beach. He was a goofy mutt, and Angela threw sticks into the water for him to fetch because he enjoyed swimming so much. As a child, Angela longed for a dog, and Fluffy served as her surrogate pet. She loved him and often pretended he was hers. She wishes she could hug him right now.

The squawk of seagulls in search of food jolt her from her memories of Fluffy. Angela shivers, turns her face toward the sun and takes a deep breath filling her nostrils with the scents of the ocean and sand. Her recollection of Fluffy has eased her tension from being in this town. Both happy and painful memories live here, buried in the recesses of her mind for several decades.

As a young child, this beach had been her playground. She and her family lived and picnicked on this shore daily when the weather permitted. She smiles, reflecting on those fun-filled days. Her smile fades, though, when thoughts of Larry resurface. It had been years since she thought of him, but the memory of Fluffy brought Larry to the forefront. Remembering him makes Angela realize that her trip is accomplishing its purpose. Larry had been a teenage neighbor who used to hang out with her older brothers, and Fluffy was his dog. Larry gave Angela piggyback rides in the water before dunking her, and he made her laugh with his crazy antics. He always treated her as if she were special. She recalls the last time she and Larry were together when she was five years old. The April sun had just started to warm Rockport on that lovely Saturday, and the residents began spending more time at the beach.

"Hello, Miss. Angela, my beautiful angel." Larry sits beside her on the sand, and Fluffy is lying in front of them, licking the girl's leg.

"Hi, Larry. What's an angel?"

"An angel is a heavenly being, one of God's helpers."

"What's a heavenly being? I don't know God."

"It doesn't matter, Little One. He knows you."

"How am I helping?"

"You're helping me. You're my special little buddy, and you make me smile when I'm with you. And Fluffy says you're beautiful, too."

"Dogs don't talk, Silly." Angela giggles at the thought.

"This one does. Where are your brothers?"

"They're doing chores, but they should be here soon. They said they wanted to go out in your boat today."

"While we're waiting for them, want to race me to the breakwater? I'll give you a head start."

"Hey, Larry!" One of Angela's teenage sisters is waving him over to her.

"Hang on I'll be right there. First, Angela and I have something to do."

Larry scoops Angela into his arms and drapes her over his shoulder. He runs to the breakwater carrying her, yelling like Tarzan, and telling her he will win the race. Angela laughs and laughs as she bobs on his shoulder while he runs.

On the evening of the next day, the sixteen-year-old Larry went out on his boat. He did not tell his parents where he was, and when he did not return home by bedtime, they called the police. Angela heard the adults in the neighborhood talking. No one understood why he had gone out alone that night and did not check the storm warnings. Nobody noticed him leave the dock, and it was odd for him to leave Fluffy at home. Because he grew-up at the ocean, Larry knew better. Still, he broke several boating safety rules. Search parties retrieved his lifeless body from the water, but Angela did not want to accept his death.

The entire neighborhood was grief-stricken and banded together to help his family through their horrific loss. Angela's mother contributed to the parade of casseroles going to Larry's house every day. She sat with Larry's mother for hours, holding her hand while she cried and cursed God. Parents hugged their children tighter and were more cautious in allowing them to go boating without an adult. Life in their seaside neighborhood lost its spark since they lost Larry.

Fluffy was inconsolable. For months, he spent his days sitting on the beach, whimpering and surveying the water in search of his master. Angela often sat with him so he was not mourning alone, stroking his thick, black coat and telling him everything will be okay. Sometimes, she cried along with him, and he licked the salt off her face from both the tears and the ocean spray. Fluffy and Angela became inseparable.

Despite the tragic loss of Larry and, in time, Fluffy, too (or, perhaps, because of them) the shore has always been Angela's favorite place. That is where she feels God's presence most and witnesses his awesomeness. Too, from the safety of the land, she can experience the reckless abandon of the swirling sea and the raw power of the pounding waves without exposing herself to their danger. Larry's tragic fate proved how merciless the ocean could be. But the reckless abandon, power, and safety combine to give her a sense of invincibility. Because fear and helplessness had filled her childhood, Angela craves that feeling and often goes to the ocean to get her fix.

Now, she attempts to immerse herself in the seaside atmosphere, hoping it will trigger more memories. She listens to the contrast between the thunder of the crashing waves and the calming rhythm of the gentler tide lapping the shore.

Nothing else compares to this stretch of beach for Angela. Most often, the seashore brings her peace and comfort akin to coming home, and she savors its tranquility. But today, a third and conflicting emotion is in the mix: fear.

Angela releases the tight grip she had on the section of her mind that has kept those early, painful memories blocked for many years, and they now flood her with the force of a tidal wave. She is choking back tears but realizes she must push forward despite her dread. Otherwise, those ghosts will haunt her forever.

With a renewed resolve and wanting to start her healing at the beginning, Angela hikes over a dune to the street where her life had begun. She needs to see their old house again, only a stone's throw up the road from the ocean. As Angela passes the Santoros' former home, she wonders if their huge, white and weather-worn house remains in their family. She wishes the Santoros were still alive and she could sit in their kitchen and visit once more, soaking up their warmth. Angela could use the comfort the elderly couple had provided in her childhood.

When Angela reaches her family's old house, only two hundred feet from the Santoros', it startles her to see they have removed the big, wrap-around porch. Angela had loved that porch, spending countless hours playing there with her siblings. Without it, the old house looks smaller than she remembered, and she feels as if she has lost an old friend. To give herself a slight protective distance, she sits on the wooden bench across the street and studies the two-story colonial her family had rented. Angela can almost hear the long-ago shouts and laughter of her siblings in the yard:

"It's my turn on the swing."

"Mom, Gino won't share!"

"Play nice, you two."

"Who wants to go swimming?"

A new, modern-design dwelling with a glass wall facing the ocean occupies the large side yard where the children once played. The intensity of her disappointment at the changes to the house and landscape surprises Angela. She feels robbed. *Get a grip, girl! That's the nature of life, always changing and evolving.*

That thought makes her wonder if she might need to change her beliefs about her childhood and how she perceived her experiences.

Angela braces herself and tries to muster her courage. *Okay, I can do this.*

She takes a deep breath, relaxing her body and mind, and wills herself to encourage and embrace more memories she had blocked. The woman insists on revisiting her childhood without limits or boundaries, facing her fears head-on and accepting the pain. Angela wants to examine the past with an adult perspective and more wisdom, knowledge, and objectivity than she had as a child. She hopes she will have compassion for the people she has resented and be able to forgive herself and others for mistakes.

While she knows she will not escape the unpleasant emotions this journey will evoke, Angela hopes the voyage will cleanse her soul and bring the peace she needs. When she embraces her decision to reexamine and accept her childhood instead of blocking and fighting it, her fear decreases.

Angela allows her mind to return to that pivotal day, July 4th of her fifth summer—the day that had started everything. Although it was long ago, she remembers the vivid events as if they were a movie playing on a screen in front of her.

2

THE MESSAGE

On this sunny Fourth of July, five-year-old Angela and her family scatter around the big front porch, stoop, and yard. Twelve of the sixteen people comprising their clan are home for the celebration. The mother of this enormous brood, Viola, has been in the hospital for the past two weeks. The oldest daughter is at home with her husband and children. Viola's eldest son is serving in the U.S. Army, and Teresa, the ten-year-old, is at her paternal aunt's house doing chores to earn a few dollars.

"When's Mom coming home?"

"When she's better." Luigi Carcieri, Viola's common-law husband, softens his tone. "The doctors are helping her, and we hope it won't take too much longer."

"Can you take me to visit her tomorrow?"

"We'll see."

"Tomorrow is Sunday so you won't have to work. I miss her."

"Yes, we all do. Tomorrow afternoon might work for a visit."

The infant lets out a small, squeaky cry, and the sixteen-year-old, Mary, picks up her baby brother from the bassinet beside her on the porch. Nine days shy of three months old, he looks so cute in his red, white, and blue outfit. While

Viola was pregnant with this baby, her oldest daughter was expecting, too. The infants, both boys, had been born a few weeks apart, making Angela's newest brother younger than his nephew.

"Evie, will you heat his bottle?" Mary asks.

"Sure."

"Can I feed him?" Angela asks. "I won't drop him."

"Okay, but you come sit next to me, and I'll hand him to you. Don't forget to hold his neck, and I'll burp him when it's time."

Angela beams as she holds her tiny brother. She is careful to keep his bottle upright, just as Mary taught her, so he does not suck air and get a bellyache. Mary, the most maternalistic of the children and Angela's favorite sibling, watches her like a hawk to make sure the baby is okay.

On this fateful day, Luigi and the older children are looking after the family in the mother's absence. As a special treat, he makes several pans of his delicious, Sicilian style pizza. Angela joins him in the kitchen. She enjoys helping, and Luigi lets her put the mozzarella on top of the homemade sauce and crust. She nibbles on the cheese as she works.

The large kitchen, a later addition to the house, heats along with the oven, and beads of sweat cover Luigi's brow, dampen his thick crop of black hair and moisten his shirt. He is an imposing presence, weighing around two-hundred-fifty pounds on a five-foot-eight frame, and his deep-set brown eyes add interest to his handsome, olive-skinned face. Luigi wipes his brow with his forearm instead of a handkerchief.

"Whew! At least the humidity isn't too bad today. I'm looking forward to my swim later. Wish I could jump in right now."

"Can I go with you, Daddy?" Angela wants to be with her father any chance she gets.

"Sure. Everyone can go."

Before long, the house smells like one of those fabulous pizzerias in the Italian section of town. When the other children get a whiff, they run into the house.

"Is that pizza we smell?"

"What makes you think so?" Luigi asks.

"Come on; we know how pizza smells."

"Then, I guess you'd better go wash your hands so you can have some."

"Yay!" They run toward the bathroom, pushing and shoving each other, unable to control their overflowing energy.

The clan is a noisy bunch as they gather at the massive table dominating the dining room that spans the full width of the house. Streams of sunlight from the room's wall of windows form yellow patterns across the table's surface. The children are eating as if they are starving and never learned table manners. Too busy shoveling pizza into their mouths, they don't even bother with their habit of talking over each other. Evie, the fourteen-year-old, voices her concern that the boys will devour everything and stakes her claim.

"Can we save two pieces for Mom and bring them to her tomorrow?"

"Save pizza for Teresa, too," chimes in Angela.

"That's a good idea," Luigi replies. "Don't worry; we have plenty. I left another pan in the kitchen."

Their father smiles when the children finish their lunch in record time. Luigi enjoys feeding people, and although they are poor, they always eat well. With satisfied bellies, they go back outside to enjoy the perfect weather and release their excess energy. Luigi sits on the front porch with many of the children while they play.

As the sun moves further west, and the afternoon wanes, the family is chattering and laughing. Their anticipation of the upcoming fireworks and the annual bonfire on the beach makes them so excited, it charges the air with electricity. Along with all the neighbors, they will be at the beach tonight for the big party.

Many of Angela's older siblings and their friends are playing a softball game in the side yard, and one teenager is pulling the two toddlers in a wagon. Addressing the ballplayers, Luigi shouts a reminder.

"Watch out for the windows!"

Angela and a few of her siblings are playing with the traditional Fourth of July sparklers on the porch. The sparklers are metal wheels with bright colors and a handle. The wheel spins round and round by squeezing the handle, and the metal rubbing against metal causes enough friction to create sparks. As a bonus, the colorful, painted design on the toys makes a mesmerizing, changing pattern as they spin. Fluffy barks and tries to bite them. The children love playing with the sparklers, and they are one of Angela's favorite Fourth of July activities.

The unfamiliar sound of a motorcycle, growing louder as it approaches, grabs the family's attention. They stop what they are doing and stare at the bike as it comes up their street. The family looks comical, frozen in mid-action as they watch and listen.

The motorcycle comes closer until it stops in front of their house. It surprises everyone when the uniformed police officer gets off his bike and climbs their front steps. He pats the heads of a few children sitting there and smiles at them as he ascends the stairs. In a somber voice, he addresses Luigi.

"Sir, can we step inside for a moment?"

"Why? What's the problem, officer?"

"Let's go inside, please."

Luigi responds by opening the screen door and gesturing the policeman into the house. The children wait on the porch, fidgeting and shushing each other, trying to hear the men's conversation. They know something is amiss. Angela wonders why the officer is here.

Is someone in trouble? Is he going to arrest one of my brothers or even Daddy?
When the policeman comes outside and leaves without looking at or addressing the children, Angela exhales. When she sees her father's face, though, the tension returns. Luigi's distress is visible when he tells the children to send their friends home and come into the house. His moist, red eyes betray his efforts to present a composed demeanor. The family gathers in the living room.

"Well?" After waiting a few moments without response, Mary asks again. "Please, you're scaring us. Tell us what's wrong."

"Your mother died this afternoon." Luigi's voice cracks, and he swallows hard. He hangs his head, then goes to his bedroom and shuts the door, leaving the children stunned and alone to handle this shocking news. Their mother had been in the hospital for treatment of the large, malignant mole on her back.

Angela had not realized the seriousness of her mother's illness and had not asked questions. She accepted her mama was sick but never expected this. The other children did not look prepared for their mother's death, either. No one could believe something as insignificant as a mole took their mama's life.

Most of the children weep upon hearing the news, and the older ones are hugging each other. A teenage brother punches the wall and runs out of the house. Evie is sobbing in a corner. Through her tears, Mary finally speaks.

"We have to let Rick know, but how can we reach him in Korea?"

"And we need to tell Millie and Teresa," Evie cries.

Angela cries, too, but does not understand why. The disruption and chaos in her house confuse her. She knows what death means because she had seen animals die, and Larry never came back when he had died. The child understands she will never see her mother again, but she cannot grasp it.

Angela's tears only come because her family is grieving, and sorrow has replaced their earlier excitement.

* * *

Teresa, who has bonded to her mother, is old enough to understand the loss and bear its full impact. Still at her aunt's house, she has not heard yet of her mother's death. Teresa tells Aunt Concetta how exciting the fireworks and bonfire scheduled for this evening are and asks to be home well before they start. In the late afternoon, after doing the housecleaning, Teresa says she feels tired, lies on the sofa, and falls asleep. The girl awakens and bolts up, crying out, "She's dead! She's dead!" Teresa's declaration occurs at the exact time her mother dies, and her aunt confirms Teresa's story. Angela believes her sister's account of the incident because she, too, has had similar unusual and inexplicable experiences.

When Teresa arrives home a short while later, she walks into a house full of crying siblings. Mary approaches her to break the news, but Teresa stops her.

"You don't have to tell me. I know Mom is dead." Her mama was only forty-two years old.

3

WHEN THEY WERE ALL TOGETHER

While sitting on the bench across from her family's former home, something baffles Angela. Although her father has always loomed large in her life, and she has a remarkable memory for everything else, she has few memories of her mother. Angela's lack of mourning when her mother died gnaws at her.

What's wrong with me? Larry's death bothered me more. I know I was young, but still, it's weird. Why wasn't I heartbroken since I remember her as a good mom? If only I had known her better!

Angela doesn't have the answers and focuses on what she knows versus getting stuck in what she does not know. She has a flashback of her mother sitting in the rocking chair, brushing her daughter's hair.

"Are you almost done, Mama?"

"Why are you in a hurry? I enjoy brushing your hair."

"How come?"

"It gives me extra time with you, Angela. Don't you enjoy it?"

"I like to sit in your lap better. Can you rock me?"

"Sure, but give me a hug first."

*   *   *

When Luigi moved in with Viola twelves years ago, she had seven children from an earlier marriage. Then, Angela's parents had seven children together. Angela was Luigi's middle child. Viola was careful not to make distinctions between her two sets of children, and she insisted they call each other sisters and brothers. She forbade them to call each other half-sisters or half-brothers.

Angela dares to dig deeper into her memories, and her first memory of her mother surfaces. One morning, while everyone is still asleep, three-year-old Angela leaves the second-floor bedroom where all eight sisters sleep three to a bed, and she shuffles downstairs. Her chubby little fingers struggle to turn the doorknob to her parents' bedroom, and she climbs atop their bed and nestles between their blanketed forms.

"Good morning, Sunshine." Daddy smiles.

Mama kisses her cheek and pulls her to her warm, soft body. The child smiles and snuggles even closer. She gets her parents to herself only on rare occasions, and she loves the attention.

Their special time is short-lived, though, because her parents must begin their day. When Luigi sits up in bed to put on his pants, Angela points to her father's private parts in innocence.

"What's that?"

Luigi gets red in the face and swears in Italian. Angela doesn't know what is wrong, but his rage frightens her, and she cries.

"She's too young to understand; she doesn't know any better." In a swift, protective gesture, her mother scoops up Angela.

"Let's go make pancakes." Mama carries her confused little girl out of the room, but Luigi's fury makes a strong impression.

Mama is nurturing, too, when the child sustains a severe injury. Angela is playing river on her bed with a few of her siblings. The game comprises jumping on the mattress and diving from one end to the other. Angela, who is either three or four years old, overshoots her mark, dives off the bed, and splits her head open on the blade of an ice skate. Blood squirts from the gash on her head and the older children scream to the parents in a panic.

"Bring her to me." Viola's tone is serious.

While a much older brother is holding Angela in his arms at the top of the stairs, she sees her parents standing below, looking concerned. Without warning, she experiences a flying sensation as her brother throws her over the stairs to her parents. Her parents catch her, but Angela screamed as she took the unexpected flight.

While her mother tries to stop the bleeding with cold, wet washcloths, her composure calms Angela. The child notices her daddy looks worried, but he only watches.

"She needs to go to the hospital for stitches." Her mother's voice sounds higher-pitched than usual.

"I don't want to go to the hospital!"

"Don't be afraid of the hospital. And don't worry; I'll stay with you while the doctors and nurses fix the cut on your head and make you better."

"Will you hold me?"

"You bet I will." Angela recalls feeling better because of her mother's presence and reassurance.

One of Angela's favorite memories from those early years is her maternal grandmother's occasional visits from Michigan. Grandma L., a slender, gray-haired woman with glasses, is of Norwegian descent. At every visit, Grandma is well-dressed and groomed in her sheer stockings, high heels, straight dark skirt, and silky pastel-colored blouse. When she walks through the door, Angela runs to her in delight, calling "Grandma!" She hugs her grandmother's legs, and the woman puts Angela on her lap, rocks her, and talks to her in a soothing voice. Grandma L. always smells of lavender. Angela loves the scent and moves in closer to enjoy it more. Occasionally, the woman sings her a melody, inserting Angela's name into the song to make her think someone wrote it just for her. While Grandma sings, Angela enjoys fingering the shiny broach pinned to her collar. She wishes her grandmother will stay with her forever and cries every time she leaves.

Grandma L. always came alone when she visited Angela's family. The children never met her husband, their maternal grandfather.

"Why doesn't our Grandpa come to visit with Grandma?" Angela looks to her mother for an answer.

"He died a long time ago before you were born."

"Why did he die?"

"He worked for the railroad and, in a terrible accident, a train ran him over and killed him."

The thought of the train accident horrified Angela. She tried not to visualize it, but it kept popping into her head over the next several weeks.

Angela has no memories of her paternal relatives before her mother's death. She does not remember them helping the family when her mother died or even being present. Her father, who had never married her mother and had seven "illegitimate" children, was the black sheep in his proud, proper family. His parents never accepted the children's mother, and they had never visited her home. As a young child, Angela was unaware of any animosity. In her world, those relatives did not exist before age five.

When they are still together before their mother's death, the family has a routine that Angela looks forward to every week. On Sunday mornings, Luigi cooks breakfast for the entire household. After they eat, Luigi gives each of the children (except the older teenagers) a nickel for allowance. The children's pattern never alters: they walk along a short, dirt pathway from their backyard to a small post office where they spend their money on penny candy. Angela picks her treats based on how many pieces she can get for a penny instead of how they taste. She always chooses the candies that are two or three pieces for one cent and comes home with a small, brown paper bagful for the nickel.

On this Sunday, they have finished breakfast, but Luigi has not yet given the children their allowance. They assemble in the small backyard and argue who will ask their father for the money.

"You go ask."

"I'm not going; you go."

Most of the children act afraid to ask him. This huge man is wearing an apron while washing the breakfast dishes. Angela can hear the water running and the clatter of the plates. She does not want to wait any longer for her candy, so she pipes up, proud to volunteer. The offer delights Angela's siblings, and they are eager to urge her forward, pushing her up the back steps.

"Hi, Daddy." The screen door slams shut as she enters the kitchen.

"Hi, Baby; do you need something?"

"Can we have our allowance? We want to get our candy."

"Oh, did I forget?" Luigi stops what he is doing and calls the children into the kitchen.

"There you go." He smiles as he places a nickel in each greedy little hand. Angela kisses her father on the cheek and cannot figure out why her siblings fear him.

But where is Mama?

The thought of her mother's absence from Angela's life even before she died brings her sister, Mary, to mind. Because she gets attention and nurturing from her, Angela attaches to her lovely, blonde-haired sister. The child lies in bed every night and calls for Mary to tuck her in, and her big sister obliges. If her sister is out on a date, Angela repeats the same statement while she cries herself to sleep. "I want Mary."

"Knock it off!" Her brothers, irritated by the continual crying, try to quiet her. Then, the only sound is Angela's whimpering.

Where is Mama? Why doesn't she come to tuck me in bed? Doesn't she hear me crying?

Besides Mary, Angela became attached to an elderly couple in the neighborhood, Mr. and Mrs. Santoro. Because Luigi speaks Italian to them, they have become close friends. Her father often brings a few of his children when he visits the couple. At every visit, the homemade Italian food cooking on their big, cast-iron stove fills their house with wonderful aromas. Mrs. Santoro carries a plate of meatballs or eggplant parmigiana and places it in front of Angela.

"*Mangia! Mangia!* You too skinny, *mangia!*"

"*Grazie.*" Daddy had taught Angela what to say, and she practiced the word.

"*Che bella bambina!*" Mrs. Santoro then pinches her cheek and plants a kiss on Angela's head.

"*Grazie.*" Angela flashes the woman a smile.

Mr. and Mrs. Santoro are generous people, and Angela enjoys visiting them, feeling welcome and comfortable there. She views them as surrogate, loving grandparents. But the little girl wonders why her mother never joins them on these visits.

One of her most memorable encounters with Mr. Santoro happened that fall. Because Angela had started kindergarten in September, her parents allowed her to go trick-or-treating with her older siblings. As they are returning home and near their house, one brother stops dead in his tracks. With eyes bulging, he points up the road and shouts.

"Look!"

A sister looks up and lets out a blood-curdling scream. In an instant, terror surges through the children's veins as they see a white, ghostly figure flying toward them. The oldest brother picks up Angela, and they run screaming for their lives, jump into Luigi's car (the closest safe place), and blast the horn. Luigi emerges from the house, and a few neighbors open their doors to see what the commotion is.

Mr. Santoro approaches them dressed in black, with even his face blackened, carrying a broom with a white bedsheet over it. He had been fluttering it above his head as a ghost. Their end of the road has no streetlights, so the children could only see a spirit flying around, not the broomstick or the man holding it. As soon as Mr. Santoro sees how terrified the children are, he pulls the sheet off the broom and shows them it was only he. Mr. Santoro apologizes to Luigi and the children, and while he says he did not intend to frighten them this much, he cannot stop laughing. Luigi laughs, too, but the children do not appreciate the humor. They are still trembling, except Angela. She knows nothing of ghosts, so she has no fear. The child thought her siblings were playing a game when they went running and screaming.

*　*　*

The next memorable event for Angela was Christmastime. This season is always exciting for the children. Decorations and treats are plentiful throughout the neighborhood and at school. Angela loves the Christmas carols, the aroma of cookies baking, and the seasonal stories her siblings read to her. But the Christmas tree impresses Angela most. Her parents' tradition is to cut a huge tree and put it up two days before Christmas. Angela enjoys the balsam scent that fills their house, and she sticks her nose into the branches every time she passes, but the tree remains unadorned when the children go to bed on Christmas Eve. When they run downstairs on Christmas morning, a radiant vision greets them. The twinkling lights, glimmering tinsel, and shiny, colorful ornaments have transformed the tree. It overwhelms and enthralls Angela, who can't stop staring at it. Too, she enjoys looking at herself in the colored glass balls and watching the candle-shaped lights containing bubbling fluid. She finds the gentle bubbling sound soothing. Angela's parents say Santa Claus decorated the tree.

During the winter, the older kids have snowball fights and build snow forts with their friends. Sometimes they go sledding, but Angela refuses to get on the sled, preferring to watch them slide down the hill. Likewise, she enjoys watching them skate, but will not risk it herself. Wintertime always brings Grandma L. for a visit, a real treat for Angela.

While thinking of treats, Angela remembers her mother's delicious baking in those early years. Mason jars, filled with preserved peaches, plums, apples, and pears from the fruit trees in their backyard, line the pantry shelves and enable her mama to make homemade fruit pies throughout the year. The sweet and inviting aroma of those baking pies often permeates the house. Mama takes the scrap pieces of dough she's trimmed and rolls them up with cinnamon and sugar. She wastes nothing. Angela makes sure she's around when those little treats come out of the oven.

By far, though, summer is the best season. Her older siblings are available to play with Angela, and the family spends most of their time at the beach and in the water. The neighborhood comes to life during this season, and they see much more of their neighbors. Everyone spends most of their time outside, which Angela loves.

Sometimes on hot summer days, the children can buy ice cream from the truck that comes through the neighborhood ringing its bell to announce its presence. Their ears perk up when they hear that sound, in anticipation that today might be the day they get lucky and can have a refreshing treat. On those days, Angela always orders a cone of rainbow ice cream. That way, she does not have to choose just one flavor but gets a sampling of several. The little girl struggles to decide most things because she fears she will make the wrong decision, but she does not regret this choice. It is real ice cream, not rainbow sherbet. Ice cream has always been her favorite treat. Fluffy likes it, too, and Angela makes sure he gets a lick when no one is looking.

When they are not at the beach, the children spend most of their time in the side yard running around, swinging on the tire hanging from the limb of one of the two enormous, ancient trees that inhabit the yard, pulling wagons, playing ball, exploring nature, and letting their imaginations run wild. One day, Luigi's second oldest child, nine-year-old Anna, spots a bird's nest in a backyard tree. She watches the nest from the ground for several days. Then, upon hearing the baby birds' squeaky chirping, she gets excited they have hatched. She climbs the tree and has a closer look. When Anna gets too close to the nest, the mama bird shrieks and the children hear a shrill cry.

"Help! Help! *Owww!*"

"What's wrong? Anna, are you okay?"

Anna is too busy screaming to answer. The protective mama bird chases Anna as she scurries to the ground, pecking on her head the entire time, while Anna yells at the top of her lungs! Her brothers find this scene hilarious and convulse with uncontrollable laughter, rolling around in the grass, holding their sides.

The side yard, too, has the family's large vegetable garden and an herb garden. Many varieties of vegetables flourish in the garden, and they help to feed so many hungry mouths. The boys are notorious for stealing vegetables from the plants before Luigi picks them. Angela, too, enjoys popping a few cherry-tomatoes into her mouth.

Their mother uses the herbs when she cooks, and she treats her children's illnesses with herbal compounds. Teresa shared the following remembrance with Angela. When the oldest son, Rick, comes home with his leg filled with splinters, his mother combines bread, milk, sugar, and herbs, and applies the mixture to the affected limb. When she removes this home remedy from his leg the next morning, the bread is full of the wood fragments that had embedded his skin. It fascinates Angela to learn their mother had a broad knowledge of the medicinal properties of herbs and, instead of a physician, she and her herbs had treated most of the children's illnesses.

Their garden is not their only source of food. The family gains a large percentage of their nutrition from the Atlantic Ocean, just at the end of their street. Fish, clams, and quahogs are plentiful. Luigi often prepares a delicious feast of steamed littlenecks, spaghetti with quahogs, fried quahogs, and Angela's favorite, stuffies. They are a mixture of chopped quahogs, Italian style breadcrumbs, grated Pecorino Romano cheese, quahog juice, and seasoning that bake in the quahog shells with a few drops of hot sauce on top. His children love this food, and several of them relish eating the littlenecks raw, sucking them and their juice right from the just-opened shells. Angela can never bring herself to eat those cold, slimy creatures, but she devours them cooked.

* * *

Also, seafood has played a significant emotional role in their lives. Throughout Luigi's life, long after the family had left that house, he dug for quahogs in the summers and, along with his wife, hosted what he called a quahog feed for his children and grandchildren. Angela remembered how drenched her father got from the steaming hot kitchen when he prepared those dinners. The work was time-consuming and labor-intensive, but it was how he showed his love. To this day, Angela cannot eat a quahog without thinking of her father and having a sense of connection and continuity.

*   *   *

Smelts are another delicacy the family gets from the ocean. They are a small fish with a mild flavor. The children enjoy eating them dredged in seasoned flour and fried. They are often a Christmas Eve staple in Italian-American households when they celebrate the Feast of the Seven Fishes. In the family's neighborhood, they get consumed several times a week in season. Neighbor families work together to fish for the smelts. The men go out in rowboats and stretch large nets between their boats to capture the tiny fish.

"Wow, they're swarming today."

"Should be quick and easy."

When the men complete their conquest by filling their nets and are ready to row back towards the shore, the call comes.

"Get ready. We're coming in."

The women and children then walk into the water up to the adults' knees, pull the smelts from the nets, and throw them into buckets. After the neighbors harvest the fish and the buckets are full, they divide the bounty amongst the participating families. The larger the family, the bigger the share, and Luigi always takes home the highest percentage of fish. The neighborhood families love smelt fishing. It not only provides them with food but working together gives them a sense of belonging to something larger than themselves and their own families. After her mother's death, a sense of belonging is something that will elude Angela for many years.

Besides being an excellent source of food, the ocean is where much of their family entertainment takes place. The children spend most sunny summer days swimming, diving off the rocks, boating, fishing, and searching for seashells. Too, they enjoy building sandcastles, skipping stones across the water's surface, playing with hermit crabs, and having picnic lunches on the beach.

Toward the end and beginning of the school years, the children wear their bathing suits to school under their clothing on hot days. When school lets out, they hop off the school bus at the top of their street, peeling off their outer clothing as they run up the road, flinging the clothes toward their yard, and rush into the water, laughing and teasing each other. Sometimes, they make it a competition.

"Last one in is a rotten egg!"

"No fair; you got a head start!"

"I did not, Miss. Slowpoke!"

*   *   *

While sitting on the bench across from her childhood home, Angela removes a few faded, black and white snapshots from her purse and studies them again. As she looks at a picture of her mother, circa 1929, she admires the woman's beauty. She was pregnant with her first child, wearing a fringed, flapper dress (reportedly, it was red), and she had bobbed hair. Her daughter marvels at how chic and *avant-garde* her mother looked! The stories her siblings shared about Viola, combined with the way her mother had lived (e.g., ignoring convention) and the things she endured (e.g., rejection and loss), lead Angela to believe her mother was a strong, independent woman who was a rebel. In another photo, her mother is wearing trousers. Again, her attire was unusual for that era.

"Go, Mom," Angela says aloud. She smiles in admiration of her mother's spunk.

With her hands cupping the few precious photos she has of her mama, droplets of happiness from her recollections escape her eyes and roll down her cheeks. Her tears come from recognizing she has many happy memories she had buried deep after tragedy struck and ripped away her innocence. She was unaware of those happy memories for most of her life. In avoiding the unpleasant and its pain, she had buried the good memories, too. Now, she has them back. Among them was the fun she and her siblings had living next to the ocean.

Alas, those laughing, carefree children were unaware of what a privileged life they lived despite their poverty, and how blessed they were before the death of their mother. They did not know what awaited them after her death. If they did, they would have been neither laughing nor carefree.

4

POSTMORTEM

Angela is too young to attend her mother's funeral, but she must endure the aftermath of Viola's death, which includes many life changes. The result of her death is as if the family is an exploding bomb and the children are the shrapnel, scattering in every direction and mere fragments of what they had been.

Angela's half-siblings leave their home after the funeral, except Evie, who stays a few weeks to help with her younger siblings. After moving into an apartment in town, they never again returned to the house where they were born and raised. Soon after their departure, the youngest of those siblings, a thirteen-year-old boy, moves to Alaska to live with his father. Around the same time, the eighteen-year-old, Robby, joins the Marine Corps.

Angela is unaware of the moves, and the changes in the household confuse the child because nobody has explained the events to her.

"Where's Mary and the rest of the kids?" Angela has been asking this question every day, and the response is always the same. "They're busy."

But today, Teresa responds to her. "Last week, they moved to a new place."

"How come? Are they coming back? Everyone is supposed to live here. I want Mary."

"But they live somewhere else now and aren't moving back. Mary and the others wanted their own apartment."

"But I need to see her. Please, I don't want everyone to go away. They didn't say goodbye to me." Angela wipes the tears now streaking her cheeks.

"It's not fair, and I'm sorry, but it'll be okay. Daddy and the rest of us are still here. Maybe we'll be able to visit Mary and the others. How about you give me a big hug, and we will go to the beach? Fluffy probably wants to see you there."

Angela falls into her big sister's arms while sobs rack her wisp of a body.

"I love you, Peanut." Teresa is rubbing her sister's back as they hug.

"I love you, too, Teresa."

For the first few weeks after their mother's death, Luigi and his children receive help from a charitable organization. Red Feather ladies come to the house every weekday to give the children breakfast, get them dressed, and babysit those too young for school. The name of these women tickles Angela, who envisions the women in hats with big red feathers protruding from them. But, to her dismay, they display no red feathers.

Theresa walks the women to the bus stop each day at 4:00 p.m. and she and Evie watch the younger children until Luigi comes home from work. Angela thinks the Red Feather women are pleasant, but nothing is the same as before her mother's death. Nobody smiles anymore, she misses her half-siblings, and her father withdraws.

Within a month of his wife's death, Luigi realizes he can no longer work and raise seven children by himself. The Red Feather ladies can offer only temporary help, and Luigi, as a laborer, cannot afford to pay babysitters or housekeepers. Soon, Angela and her siblings, along with their father and

Aunt Concetta, are in a courthouse in the capital city. The children know their aunt, who must have had a role in their lives, but this day is Angela's first memory of her.

At the courthouse, everyone speaks in hushed voices, and it has the same air of reverence as attending church. The family wears their best Sunday clothes, many made by their mother. Katherine, a toddler, yells, and the sound ricochets off the marble walls, floors, and high ceilings in the enormous lobby. Several "*Shhhs*" from family and strangers scold the child. Angela gazes in awe at the lovely artwork. The grandeur around her impresses the five-year-old, who has never seen such splendor. The girl has her first elevator ride to the second floor, but that is unimpressive. Someone is telling the children not to be afraid.

Afraid of what? Why are we here?

The Carcieri children do not meet with a judge or enter the actual courtroom. They sit on a hard, wooden bench in the lobby outside the chambers for what seems an eternity to Angela. To entertain herself, she clicks her brown leather shoes on the marble floor, tapping the beat to "Twinkle Twinkle Little Star" playing in her head. The adults shush her, too. At last, her father comes out and goes to his children. Luigi's voice shakes and is much softer than usual as he tells them what will happen.

"Kids, you're moving to a new house. I can't go with you, but it'll only be for a while, then we'll be together again." For a moment, Angela thinks they will live with Mary and the others.

"Where are we going?"

"It's a big place with lots of other children to play with."

"But I can't go. Fluffy needs me. What will happen to him?"

"Fluffy will be fine. Larry's parents are his family, and they take good care of him. You know that."

"Can you bring him to visit me?"

"We'll see."

"What if we don't like it? I can take care of the little ones," Teresa says.

"I can't afford to keep the house anymore, and you need to be at school. It's for the best. Donald and Katherine will live with a nice foster family, and the rest of you will be together in another place." Luigi reassures no one but himself.

Auntie Concetta tries to comfort the confused and upset children, telling them everything will be okay, then she and Luigi kiss them goodbye.

"We'll see you soon when we visit."

The bewildered children watch as Luigi walks away. Then, an unfamiliar woman, likely a social worker, escorts Angela and her one-year-younger sister, Margie, to a car. The stranger does not introduce herself or explain where they are going. Though the events of this day confuse her, Angela is not afraid. The child does not know what will happen next and is trying to put the pieces together, assuming she is going to the new house her daddy mentioned. Angela wonders where the rest of her siblings are. She had learned at a young age that she should not ask too many questions. Also, keeping Angela and Margie unaware of their destination is best.

5

THE CHILDREN'S CENTER

Angela is hyper-alert when she arrives at their destination and tries to assess the place. As they drive through the large gates, her eyes dart everywhere. She sees no evidence of warmth or coziness. Strangers, both children and adults, are everywhere. The little girl was expecting a house, not these large stone and brick buildings. Angela doesn't believe they will live here and decides they are only stopping for a while.

"Where are we?" Angela asks. The woman is parking in front of a brick building.

"This is the Children's Center."

"Is it a school? I thought we were going to our new house."

"This is the state orphanage. It's where you will live. Come with me; We'll put your things in your room." Angela is unsure she wants to exit the car.

The woman takes the sisters to a large room with rows of twin beds lining two opposite walls. When Angela discovers she and Margie will bunk next to each other, she exhales a bit of the tension causing her headache. The girls put their belongings into the single drawer assigned to each then head outside to join the other children from their building. No one introduces them. A few adults say a smileless hello, and others show no awareness of their presence, acting as if they are invisible. Many of the children stare at them.

I want to go home!

Angela latches onto Margie's hand. Much of Angela's time at the orphanage is routine, such as attending school, but specific incidents and people cement into her memory.

Ruth, a housemother, is most unforgettable. She is an enormous woman, weighing between 350 and 400 pounds. Angela sees Ruth as a giant, but the woman is only around five-feet-five-inches tall. She has short, jet-black hair that stands in stark contrast to her pale white skin. Her unattractive face looks hardened and has a significant number of moles and blemishes. Ruth is an unhappy woman. Her smile is sinister instead of expressing joy, and she takes pleasure in the power she has over the helpless state wards, whom she loathes. With justification, Angela lives in fear of the woman.

They serve thick, pasty, unsweetened oatmeal for most breakfasts at the Children's Center, and Angela hates it. When Ruth first notices Angela is not eating the food, she approaches her.

"Why aren't you eating?"

"It tastes yucky."

Ruth slams a paddle onto the table, narrows her eyes, and barks at the child. "Well, that's just too bad. Now, eat it!"

Angela tries to force herself to swallow the cereal, but she keeps gagging, which enrages Ruth. She hits Angela on the back with the thick wooden paddle she carries, a rectangular piece of solid wood with a handle carved into it. Overall, the dreaded instrument is around fourteen inches long, four inches wide, and one and one-half inches thick. Ruth uses it to terrorize the children. That paddle plays a leading role in Angela's nightmares.

"Don't you dare throw up, or I'll make you eat that, too." She is looming over the trembling child and waving her paddle with menace. Angela knows Ruth will carry out her threat, so, with hands shaking, she chokes down the breakfast through her sobs. In her mind, she pleads for her stomach to settle and begs not to vomit.

From then on, every time they serve oatmeal, Ruth sits next to Angela, holding her paddle and threatening to use it if the child does not eat faster. Angela tries to eat quickly, but when she is too slow for Ruth, she receives another whack with the paddle on her arm, back or thigh. Never again has Angela eaten oatmeal since leaving the orphanage so many years ago, and the mere thought of it still makes her cringe.

Another incident with Ruth left a permanent scar on Angela's psyche. For a special outing, children from the Center are traveling by bus to visit a nearby U.S. Navy base. When the buses arrive, sailors board the bus in pairs to choose the children they will tour the facility with and visit for an hour or two. Angela and her sister, Margie, are sitting together, waiting for someone to choose them.

When only a handful of children remain on their bus, the two sisters are still waiting. The circumstances remind Angela of being the last child picked for an impromptu, schoolyard baseball game. But this rejection is not a game.

"I'll bet no one will pick those two." Ruth is referring to Angela and Margie as she jerks her head in their direction and snickers. She turns to the sisters.

"Nobody wants you." Then she laughs, looking directly at them. Ruth takes pleasure in her cruel comments, but Margie cries. Angela tries to console her, putting her arm around her sister.

"Don't worry; someone will pick us." But Angela holds her breath every time a sailor enters the bus.

At last, two sailors come aboard and choose the sisters. The children breathe easier and smile at each other. As the girls are walking up the aisle, Angela hears Ruth talking to the woman beside her, in a sincere tone. "Boy, I'm surprised. I thought no one would want them."

35

Angela's smile disappears and, for the first of many times to come, she believes she is inferior, and because others can see something is wrong with her, although she does not know what, it humiliates her. She hopes Margie did not hear what Ruth said.

Angela feels ashamed, too, because of a daily practice she must endure. Life at the Center is so regulated that they schedule toilet time. In Angela's unit, which houses children from ages three through six, around eight child-size toilets stand in a row in a large room. They are on a platform, requiring the children to climb two or three stairs. The platform saves the workers from the repeated bending needed to wipe the children when the toilets are low enough for the smallest children to reach.

Boys and girls use the bathroom together. When a child finishes eliminating, he or she must call out the number one or number two, so an attendant can unroll the needed amount of toilet tissue. For number one, they hand the children tissue to wipe themselves. For number two, a worker cleans the children regardless of whether they can do it themselves. Every day, it mortifies Angela to have to remove her panties in front of others, more so boys, sit on a toilet calling out what she has done, and have someone wipe her bottom as if she were a baby. She dreads having to call out number two and is fervent in hoping Ruth will not attend her. At only five and a half years old, Angela experiences shame daily and resents this toileting practice in silence.

*   *   *

The children from the Center attend the local public schools. Angela, whose birthday is in December, makes the end-of-the-year cutoff to enter first grade that September and is the youngest child in her class. Margie is in kindergarten, so Angela is alone at school. In inclement weather, the children from the Center sit on the corridor floors until the bell rings for class. They are unsupervised, but if things get too loud, a teacher comes out and shushes them.

One large and older girl attends the same school. Angela, despite her young age, is aware this girl has a mental disability. In hindsight, Angela realizes the girl had a cognitive and developmental impairment. Too, she is violent and often hits the other children for no understandable reason. Angela tries to avoid the girl, but she seeks Angela out and gives her a whack or two. The first time it happens, Angela's instinct instructs her not to strike back. The assault hurts, and she cries, but nobody helps. When it keeps happening, Angela tells the teacher.

"Even though I try to stay away from her, she finds me and hits me every day. Can you please make her stop?"

"The girl has a problem and can't help it. You should be nice to her."

Angela is not one to argue or plead her case, and she resigns herself to the attacks. The school staff does not monitor, restrain, punish, or remove the girl to protect the other children. Angela is glad the girl is not in her classroom, but almost daily throughout the first grade, the girl assaults Angela either in the recess yard or corridor.

Angela's sixth birthday passes without acknowledgment or celebration. Except for Margie, who shares the same unit, Angela does not recall seeing her siblings much at the orphanage. She misses her family and only remembers her father and Aunt Concetta coming to visit once or twice. When he visits, her other siblings living at the Center are with him. It thrills Angela to see their familiar, friendly faces. She gives Luigi a big hug and tells him how happy she is to be with him. She notices someone is missing.

"Where's Fluffy? Is he okay?"

"He's fine, but he couldn't come today."

"Will you give him a hug for me?"

"Well, I don't live in the old house anymore, but I'll try to see him when I visit the Santoros."

"I wish I could see the Santoros, too. When can we go home?"

"Pretty soon."

Angela cannot understand why she can't leave with him right then. She misses Fluffy. The child cries after her father departs. She does not allow herself to weep when they say goodbye because she does not want Luigi to be sad. That little girl tells no one how horrible life is at the orphanage, how Ruth and the girl at school abuse her, how their caretakers do not give the children any attention or show them affection, or how much she yearns to escape.

On a bright, frigid and blustery Saturday in February, the workers at the Center take the children sledding. To Angela's dismay, Ruth is attending the children from her unit. Atop the huge hill on the Center's property, most children are boisterous and laughing, sledding down the hill and running back up again, having a great time. Angela stands alone, watching everyone else have fun. Ruth approaches her.

"Why aren't you sledding?"

"I don't know how."

"What do you mean, you don't know how? Just get on the sled and go."

"But I don't know how to steer it; I'll crash."

"What, are you stupid? You pull the rope in the direction you want to go."

"No, I only want to watch." Angela's stomach churns.

"Stop being a baby. Now get on the sled."

"Please, I don't want to go."

"I didn't ask you if you wanted to, did I?"

Ruth pulls Angela by the arm with a rough jerk and forces her onto the sled, despite the child's protests. Angela is trying to fight back the panic and tears, and she thinks of something that might help.

"Wait! Can someone come with me on the sled?"

"No, don't be such a chicken!"

Ruth then gives the sled a forceful shove, and the child, with eyes bulging, heart racing, and every muscle in her body contracting, screams as she flies down the huge hill. Angela can see she will crash, but the panic paralyzes her. The child hears the horrible *whack* as the sled smashes into the tree right before it knocks her unconscious. She wakes up in the infirmary, and Angela sports a red, bruised egg on her forehead for a while. Ruth never apologizes, and Angela never gets on a sled again.

Because of her self-consciousness and timidity, Angela does not speak much and is a loner. She has made no friends here because she is so withdrawn, and she trusts no one. Although having Margie with her gives Angela comfort, she believes she has responsibility for her younger sister, so she does not confide in her or see her as a companion. Angela cannot recall a single act of kindness or warmth from any adult at the Center, and these detached caretakers do not even try to help her.

Still, the child never harbors anger toward her father, Ruth, the girl at school who hits her, or anyone else. She hates her circumstances and wishes her life were different, but she has no anger. Her life defeats her. From the time she arrives at the orphanage until after she leaves, Angela is a lonely, powerless, self-conscious, and depressed little girl, who does not feel the least bit blessed.

In the spring after her sixth birthday, around ten months after arriving, Angela leaves the state orphanage. The social worker tells her and Margie they will live with a lovely foster family. Angela doubts the people will be "lovely," and she wonders, again, why she and her siblings cannot go back home with their father and live with their own family. It is long past the soon Luigi promised. Regardless, Angela reasons the new home is unlikely to be any worse than the Children's Center.

6

THE WILSONS

"This is Mr. and Mrs. Wilson," announces the social worker. "They're your new foster parents."

"Well, hello! We're glad you're here." Joe Wilson has a friendly face.

"It will be fun having little girls in the house, again." Lena Wilson speaks as this middle-aged couple greets Angela and Margie with warm, welcoming smiles. Their five children are smiling, too.

Why are they so happy? They don't even know us.

"I'm Jane." Their gorgeous fourteen-year-old offers her hand to shake, and Angela waits a moment but takes it. Mr. Wilson introduces the rest of their family: a six-foot-tall son who, they report, is not home much; their engaged daughter (who is always with her fiancé when she is not at work); another teenage son; and eight-year-old Ray.

"Hi." Angela and Margie are holding hands for mutual support.

"Well, it looks like you're all set here. I'll be by next week to check on you. Don't look so scared; you will be fine." The social worker pats Angela's head as she leaves.

"Come on, girls. Do you want to see the house? Then I'll fix a nice lunch." With a smile, Lena takes Margie's hand and shows the girls around their two-story bungalow in the working-class neighborhood. Angela and Margie will share a bedroom on the first floor, off the kitchen. Their room was a dining room before they arrived and has no doors on it, just archways; one adjoins the kitchen, and the other leads into the living room. A bedroom to themselves, even without doors, delights Angela. She thinks it will be much better than sleeping in the orphanage dormitory.

Angela suspects the family at first, but in no time she sees they are genuine. She warms up to them and enjoys living in a house instead of an institution. Life with the Wilsons is pleasant, and Angela learns to laugh again. The girls eat their meals with the rest of the clan, and they do not force the girls to eat things they dislike. Everyone discusses their lives, just as a real family. They always include Angela and Margie in their conversations and show interest in them. The sisters want to belong somewhere and to someone so, at their request, Mr. & Mrs. Wilson allow their new foster children to call them Mommy and Daddy, which gives the girls a sense of normalcy.

Jane, the fourteen-year-old, takes an interest in Angela, who admires the teenager because she is beautiful and dresses in the latest fashion. But the attention she gives Angela is what endears her to the child.

"Do you want to come with me to my room, and I'll fix your hair?"

"Can you make it nice like yours?"

"With your pretty face, I can't miss." Jane takes Angela to her room and sits her before the dresser mirror. "Do you want it pulled back, or hanging loose?"

"Whatever way you think is best."

After brushing Angela's hair, Jane pulls several strands to one side and fastens them with a red barrette. Then she opens a tube of pale lipstick.

"Do you want to try this?"

"Yes, please. Will I get in trouble?"

"No way. Mom will understand. What do you think? You look amazing, right?"

"Wow! Thank you so much. I love it!"

"Now, for the finishing touch." Jane sprays perfume on Angela's arm and rubs her wrists together.

"Tomorrow, I can polish your fingernails."

"Yes, please." Angela wants to pinch herself to be sure she is not dreaming.

Soon, Angela becomes Janes shadow. They go for long walks through the cemetery and by the river, sometimes packing a lunch. Several times, Jane and a boyfriend meet at the river and kiss. Jane even smokes a forbidden cigarette a few times. Angela keeps her promise to Jane and tells no one. Jane is appreciative and spoils her little sidekick. Sometimes, they get dressed up in their Sunday clothes and take the bus downtown to go shopping, just her and Jane, causing Angela to believe she is special. Starving for attention and affection, the little girl soon comes to love Jane.

The family has a player piano, which plays tunes when you insert a paper scroll with a pattern of holes punched into it, similar to an old-time IBM card. This hole-pattern directs the instrument to strike specific notes, and the keys move as it plays.

Ray Wilson, one year older than Angela, is fun and he and the girls get along well.

"Come on; I'll teach you how to play the piano." He and Angela sit at the piano bench.

"Okay. So here is how you put a scroll into the piano. It plays the music. Now you try."

Angela copies what Ray showed her, and the music plays.

"Watch me." Ray runs his fingers over the piano keys as if he were playing the piano. "I'll play the keys on this side, and you play them on that side."

The two new friends so enjoy playing the piano and pretending they are real musicians on a gig. It becomes a ritual for the duo to play the piano after church on Sundays and entertain the family until dinner is ready. They even bow to the family's applause when they finish playing.

Ray, Margie, and Angela play many games in the backyard, too, such as Cowboys and Indians, Tag, or Hide and Seek. There is a small shed in the yard that the children use for a playhouse where they host pretend tea parties. Although Ray prefers rough-and-tumble activities, he is a good sport and attends the girls' tea parties.

"Do you want one lump or two?" Angela is holding an empty plastic sugar bowl over Ray's empty plastic teacup.

"Two, please. Do I have to hold my pinky finger out when I drink the tea? I don't want to look like a sissy."

"You can hold it any way you want."

"Okay. Where's the pastry with my tea?"

"Coming right up sir, fresh from the oven."

Ray often walks to school with the girls, and he tells the other children that Angela and Margie are his sisters. His personality reminds Angela of his father.

Joe Wilson is the kindest man she has ever known. Soft-spoken, gentle, and always smiling, the children love being around him. He devotes himself to his family and is hardworking. His day job is with the telephone company, and he is the trombone player in a band at night. Mrs. Wilson is a homemaker, so Joe carries the lion's share of responsibility for the family's financial support.

Civic-minded Joe belongs to several organizations and takes part in many charities. One community event he spearheaded is a Memorial Day parade benefitting a children's hospital. Joe and his children march in that parade as clowns, with Joe playing his trombone and making the spectators laugh. When Angela finds out, she pleads with Joe for days to let her be a parade clown, too, but he refuses.

"Maybe next year, when you're older."

Angela tells Jane. "Dad won't let me be in the parade. He says I'm too young." Jane decides to plead Angela's case, and Angela listens to their conversation.

"Dad, you need to let Angela be a clown this year."

"She's way too young. I don't think she can walk that far; it's a long parade route."

"Angela will be fine. We walk all the time, and she never gets tired. I'll walk next to her and make sure she's okay. Please, Dad? It will mean so much to her."

"Well, I guess it'll be okay if you watch her."

When Angela hears Joe's agreement, she is beyond excited, and gives Jane a big hug, thanking her many times. During the parade, Angela has one of the best times of her life! The crowd enjoys the smallest clown, who loves the attention. Every time she pulls out the pictures and sees such a tiny girl in a big, red clown nose and small, red circles painted on her cheeks, Angela giggles. Her experience as a clown will become one of her favorite childhood memories.

An admirable man, Joe spends his rare free time with his family and does any leisure activities with them. He does not belong to a bowling league, play golf, or go out with friends for a few beers, or even take time for himself. The man spends every waking hour being productive, and he always helps others.

Mr. Wilson watches only one television show: an evening news broadcast called the *Camel News Caravan*. John Cameron Swazey, the sole newscaster, has a distinctive voice that Angela enjoys. Every weekday evening, the family sits around the living room watching that one, fifteen-minute broadcast on the first television Angela has ever seen. It was a large, wooden piece of furniture with a small round screen only ten or twelve inches in diameter.

On weekends during the summer, Joe takes the children to the beach, park or zoo. Every Sunday morning, the family goes to church services together, and Joe often takes the family for Sunday afternoon car rides to get ice cream.

One of Angela's favorite activities is doing errands with Joe on Saturdays. She loves spending time with him and riding in the open bed of his pickup truck. Angela enjoys the sense of freedom it gives her, and the wind blowing through her hair is exhilarating. As they ride along the road, Angela waves at strangers as if she were royalty, smiling ear-to-ear.

A man of deep religious beliefs, Joe is the first person to introduce Angela to a personal God and ignite the first spark of her faith. A few days after arriving at the Wilson home, Joe takes Angela by the hand and walks her up the aisle of the local Roman Catholic church where he is a member. The empty church is enormous, lovely, and so quiet the click-clacking of their footfalls on the marble floor sounds intrusive and disruptive to the serene atmosphere. Joe and Angela sit in a front pew, and Angela spots the life-sized statues at the side altars.

"Who are they?" She had been to church a few times when she lived with her parents, but her family never discussed religion, and God had no meaning for her.

"They are just statues, but they represent the Holy Family. When you have a picture of someone, the picture is not the person; it just represents them. It's the same with statues. Those statues represent the baby Jesus with his parents, Mary and Joseph, and Jesus is the Son of God."

"But you said Joseph was his father. Who's God?"

"God is everybody's father. He is your daddy in heaven."

People had told Angela her mother was in heaven, too. She is not sure she likes heaven or God. Joe continues. "He loves you very much."

This revelation is the first time Angela ever remembers being told someone loves her, and it delights her. The notion of God confuses her, but she wants to know more, and Joe wants to educate her.

Soon after coming to stay with the Wilsons, Angela learns more about God when they enroll her in their church's parish school. The teachers are nuns, and religion classes occur daily. She has to finish the last few months of first grade in her new school. In the fall, she will begin second grade and prepare for her First Communion.

* * *

Angela loves being in school. She craves knowledge and cannot get enough. Even doing her homework is enjoyable, and Angela excels in her classes. Her teachers like her and often praise her work. The girl's ability to do well in academics makes Angela hope she might not be so defective as she had thought.

But when she has an accident in school one day, it threatens her newfound confidence. Angela needs to go to the bathroom but decides she should wait until after the morning devotions. When her class is kneeling in the aisles of their classroom for prayer, each student next to his/her desk, Angela's need becomes urgent. The girl cannot just walk out, and she cannot interrupt the prayer by asking for permission. She scolds herself for not going earlier, as she squirms and tries to hold the urgency at bay. The prayers drag on forever, and to her horror, Angela pees on the floor. When they get up, the puddle is impossible to ignore.

Her first-grade teacher addresses the class.

"Someone earlier spilled a drink in the first row. Will everyone in that row help clean the floor?"

"Yes, Sister."

"Okay, the rest of you turn to your math workbooks and do the problems on page thirty-eight while I work with the helpers."

Sister then goes into the hallway with the children who are helping, assigning them to fetch cleaning supplies. When the others are out of earshot, she addresses Angela.

"I have a spare pair of panties for you in this bag. Go to the lavatory, clean yourself, and put on the dry underwear. You can use the bag they're in to hide your wet ones."

"Thank you, Sister."

"Don't forget to wash your legs, too. When you're done, bring the mop from the janitor's closet, so the others will think that's where you were."

Angela had not been sitting, so her dress is not wet. She is most grateful for her teacher's help, but she worries the other children might know the truth and laugh at her. Not one classmate ever mentions the incident.

Lena Wilson, likewise a dear and kind person, is a sickly woman and not active. Except for church and the Sunday afternoon rides, she leaves the house only on rare occasions. Lena often sits on the front porch in her rocking chair in the good weather, talking to the neighbors, watching the passersby, and munching on cheese puffs. Several times a week during the summer, her foster mother sends Angela to buy those crunchy snacks at the small neighborhood store. Lena always thanks Angela and offers her the orange-colored treats. The girl knows how much Mrs. Wilson loves her cheese puffs, and she does not want to take any away from her, so Angela limits herself to two pieces when offered.

Once in a while, when Angela goes to the store to fetch the snacks, Lena tells her she may get herself a five-cent ice milk bar. Angela so enjoys eating the chocolate first, then sucking on the frigid, creamy, vanilla center, trying to make it last as long as possible. The child knows she is fortunate to have such a treat.

No one had ever disclosed the name of Lena's illness, but Angela realizes she has emotional problems. Many days, Lena looks sad and cries for no understandable reason. Angela sympathizes with Lena and talks to her on those blue days, hoping she will help Lena feel better. Sometimes Lena gets upset when her husband has an evening music gig. One day, when Mrs. Wilson is angry, Angela asks her something, and the woman yells at her. This outburst is unlike Lena.

"Get out of the way!" Lena pushes the child.

"I'm sorry, Mommy; I didn't mean to get in your way." Angela's eyes fill with tears and, right away, Lena cries.

"You did nothing wrong. I don't know why I yelled or pushed you; I'm so sorry."

"It's okay, Mommy. Don't cry." Lena gives Angela a tight hug and cries more.

Angela dislikes seeing Lena upset, so she tries to make her laugh and comfort her. She sits with Lena whenever Joe works at night. At a young age, Angela has a keen sensitivity to others' emotions and strong empathy for them.

"Are you sure you're only six years old?"

"No, I'm just pretending."

They both laugh. Lena always thanks Angela for helping her, then hugs her. That physical affection is much needed, and the child savors it.

For the past week, local news and weather programs have been discussing a big storm coming their way. Lena and Joe lean in closer and turn up the volume on the radio as the weathermen forecast a brutal hurricane and predict it will hit the northeast within the next week.

Their state is right in its path. The reporters urge the citizens to take precautions and prepare for the worst, and the administration has arranged temporary shelters in case of an emergency. Though the Wilsons say nothing to the children of the storm, Angela can sense their anxiety. While she has never experienced a hurricane, she understands they are dangerous.

Hurricane Carol hits their state on schedule. Angela hears the howling wind and sees trees ripped from their roots and toppled by the force of the raging gale. When she witnesses streets flooding, power lines downed, and the entire town in darkness except for candles and flashlights, she hunches in a corner, trembling and hugging her knees. Mr. and Mrs.

Wilson huddle the children together in the basement, assure them they will protect them, comfort them, and calm Angela and Margie enough for the girls to fall asleep.

The worst of the hurricane is over by the next morning. The disheveled condition of the neighborhood astonishes Angela when she arises and looks out the window. Debris is everywhere. After breakfast, Mrs. Wilson sends Angela to the neighbors across the street to ask if they are okay or need something. She cautions the child to look for and avoid any wires on the ground. Mrs. Wilson and Angela are both relieved the storm injured none of their family, friends, or neighbors. The worried girl prays there won't be any more hurricanes.

In second grade, Angela learns more about God, and she enjoys the lessons. It piques her interest when her teacher discusses angels. Sister says they are messengers of God, sent to earth to help us—the same thing Larry told her. The thought of having her guardian angel by her side comforts the child, and she finds the similarity to her name amusing. God can use people to be angels on earth, she says, people who help those in need on God's behalf. Larry said Angela was his angel. The little girl hopes she can help someone else who needs her and meet angels of her own.

Angela continues to excel in her academics and places first in her class. Her grades are bolstering her confidence, and her self-esteem is better than it ever was. Thus, it devastates her when, halfway through the school year, Angela sees the lone B on her report card amidst straight As. Throughout her short school career, her report card contained only As, so a B is foreign to her. Angela fears her grade is terrible and cries the entire way home from school.

Now the Wilsons won't want me anymore.

Angela is glad she is wrong. The Wilsons tell her the report card is excellent and, while a B is less than an A, her grade is still above average. Mrs. Wilson laughs and says she used to get Ds, and a B would have thrilled her. Their reassurance is a relief, but Angela determines never to get another B. Her entire sense of self-worth depends upon her performance. Angela bears the massive burden of perfectionism when she is such a young child. The girl is desperate to prove she is worthwhile and not deficient, and nothing short of perfection will do. Her compulsivity helps Angela control the anxiety that arises when she is in danger of looking inadequate.

* * *

The young girl loves the Wilson family and living with them. Angela feels as if she is living a fairytale because her life here is so much better than the Children's Center. This child is secure, loved, and has never been happier, causing her to fear it will end. Because she knows the Wilsons are not her natural family, she is insecure. Once, trying to allay her fears, Angela questions Lena.

"Can Margie and I stay here forever, or will you send us away?"

"You can stay as long as you want. The only time I will ever let you go is if your Dad takes you back to live with him."

"I don't think he will." Angela has her fingers crossed behind her back.

"Well, he might get married someday, and then maybe he'd be able to take you back home."

Angela does not verbalize it, but she hopes with everything she has that will not happen.

Once in a while, Luigi comes by for a brief visit with his daughters, but he never takes them anywhere, and they never see their siblings. Several times, the Wilsons tell the girls their father is coming, and they await him with much excitement. Hours pass, and he never shows. After many disappointments, Angela stops getting excited when she hears her father is coming for a visit. She is tired of waiting for Luigi.

51

One particular incident is upsetting for Angela. Today is her seventh birthday. Luigi has phoned saying he is coming over after work. This birthday differs from her ignored sixth birthday at the Children's Center. The Wilsons present a birthday cake for her at dinner, sing "Happy Birthday," and give her a gift. The celebration is fun, convincing Angela they care. But she keeps wondering if Luigi will show. She wants him to have a piece of her cake.

Again, they wait and wait. Angela keeps looking out the window to see if his car is coming. The Wilsons allow the girls to stay up past their bedtime to await their father's arrival. But tonight is a school night, so when he continues not to show, the Wilsons send the children to bed. Angela overhears Lena talking to Joe.

"How that man keeps disappointing those girls is pathetic. I'd like to give him a piece of my mind!"

"Now, Lena, we don't know why he didn't come. I'm sure he has a good reason. He could be at work or have car trouble. I'm sure he'll call when he can."

"This isn't the first time he's done this, and it's not right!"

Around 11:00 pm, Angela awakens and sees her father sitting beside her on the bed. "Happy birthday. I'm sorry that I'm late." He pulls an unwrapped string of children's imitation pearls out of his coat pocket and gives it to Angela as a present. Angela is glad her father showed at last, and she thanks him, but she is angry at him at the same time. "I was at work. That's why I'm so late." But when Luigi leans in to kiss her goodnight, and the repulsive smell of alcohol wafts over her, Angela knows he is lying.

For Angela, experiencing anger toward her father is progress. In the past, when rage was the most fitting emotion for her, Angela could only experience sadness. Anger was too dangerous. Now, because she is secure in her current home, she no longer fears her wrath, can accept it, and experience it.

One day, Luigi came to visit, accompanied by a strange woman.

"Guess who this woman is!" Angela wonders why her father is so excited, and she stares at the woman in silence. Mrs. Wilson, trying to help, interjects by addressing Angela.

"Do you remember what I told you about ever leaving me?" Angela's heart sinks.

"This is Alice. She's your new mother," Luigi announces.

What? My mother? I don't even know her!

Alice smiles too much, is over-friendly, and tries to hug the girls. Angela glares at her. She does not want a new mother. She wants Lena Wilson to keep being her mother.

"How old are you?" Angela is scowling.

"I'm thirty-seven years old."

"Why are you here?"

"Angela, we need to remember our manners," Lena says.

"I'm sorry; I just don't know why she's here."

"Your dad and I got married this week, and I couldn't wait to meet you. I love children and only married your dad because he has kids."

"Don't you have any children of your own? You're old enough."

"No, I never had kids, but I always wanted them. That's why I'm so excited to be your new mother."

Right away, Angela dislikes her. The woman sounds insincere and shows no concern for or sensitivity to the children and what meeting her means to them. Alice centers the conversation around herself and what she wants and feels. She does not ask the girls what they think or want, and she does not find out who they are.

"Do we have to go live with you now?" Angela's tone is begrudging, but her stomach is wreaking havoc. She does not want to hear the answer.

"Not yet, but we hope it won't be too long. We only have a two-room apartment, and we need to save money so we can get a place big enough for the whole family. It will be soon, though."

Angela knows what Luigi's "soon" means, and his response relieved her. She knows she will not leave for a long time. This time, she is glad to wait for Luigi.

Now that her father has Alice to help him, he takes his children to spend biweekly Saturdays at his apartment. Angela loves being with her siblings again. Alice talks sweetly to the children, and she cooks the delicious Italian food Luigi taught her to make. The children have fun in their tiny apartment comprising a kitchen and a living room/bedroom combination. The bath is at the end of the long public hallway, and every tenant on that floor shares it. Angela looks forward to those visits and becomes more attached to Luigi, her siblings, and even Alice. She knows she is with her real family, and they will always be her family no matter what happens.

On most of their Saturday visits with Luigi, he takes his children to visit his parents at their home for around an hour. Then they stop by Auntie Concetta's house. Luigi's siblings visit their parents on the weekends, too, so Angela becomes familiar with many of her paternal cousins, aunts, and uncles. Luigi told Angela that both her grandparents came from the Naples region of Italy. Along with their daughter, Concetta, they emigrated to the United States around 1910. Their seven younger children were born in America.

In the warm weather, as Angela walks toward the back of her grandparents' house, she always spots her Nonno in his garden. He grows vegetables and prized roses and tends both with meticulous devotion. She smells those amazing blossoms long before she spots her grandfather. Nonno has a grape arbor, too, and uses the harvest to make homemade wine, which the men in the family enjoy. When Angela's father and uncles praise his wine, her grandfather beams.

The family sits together in the kitchen when they visit, and when Nonno finishes tending his vegetables and roses, he sits in his comfy chair in the room's corner. Every time they see Nonno, he gives each grandchild a quarter and gets a kiss on the cheek for his generosity. Twenty-five cents is big money to Angela and, while the adults are chatting, she plans how she will use her small fortune. She always saves a portion.

Angela takes a liking to her grandfather, who is closer to her height than the other adults. Despite his small stature, he looks distinguished with his gray hair and eyeglasses, and he smells of soap and herbs. He speaks only a few words in broken English with a heavy accent. The adults converse in Italian, and Angela often wishes she could understand what they are saying. Her father only speaks English to his children, but Angela wants to learn Italian so she can know why everyone is so animated. She can grasp the hand gestures, though.

At Christmastime, Angela longs for a teenage doll she saw in a magazine. It comes with a small trunk for the toy's wardrobe and accessories, such as a hairbrush, purse, and jewelry. Angela loves the thought of brushing the doll's hair and changing its outfits. When Mrs. Wilson asks her what she wants, she describes the toy in precise detail. On Christmas morning, her gift from the Wilsons is a game Angela likes and appreciates.

"Wait until you see what your father got you for Christmas!" Mrs. Wilson is full of enthusiasm this morning.

"I can't wait!" Angela knows what the gift must be and tries to contain her excitement.

Her father picks her up around 10:00 a.m. to spend the day with him, Alice, and her siblings. Everyone is excited. Angela cannot wait to play with her new doll. Before going to his apartment, they make the usual rounds to the Carcieri grandparents, then Auntie Concetta.

Their kind aunt is the only relative who gives Luigi's children each a small Christmas present, and Angela appreciates the new book she receives. The woman's genuine warmth toward the children touches her. Too, Auntie Concetta makes the most delicious Italian Christmas cookies piled high on a tray on the kitchen table. She invites the children to help themselves, and they dig into the cookies. Angela's favorites are the almond biscotti and the struffoli. Angela could eat fistfuls of them, but she remembers to be polite. She takes only two.

When they arrive at Luigi's apartment, each of the children has a Christmas present from Santa, and one from Luigi and Alice awaiting them beneath a small, decorated tree. Angela unwraps the gift from Luigi and Alice with great care and excitement, expecting the doll she's been longing for beneath the paper. As she pulls the paper away, she sees an infant doll wearing a diaper and a blanket. It has a baby bottle, one diaper change, and no hair. Her heart sinks.

"Is that the doll you wanted?" Luigi asks.

"Yes, it's just what I wanted." Angela flashes her father a big smile.

"Good. I figured it was the right one. Mrs. Wilson said you wanted a doll you could change."

"Yes. I love it!"

When she gets back home that evening, she shows Lena her doll.

"Oh, no! We bought the doll you wanted, but when your father told us he wanted to get it, we returned it. We explained what you wanted, but maybe he got confused."

"It's okay." Angela is disappointed but does not mind. She knows her father meant well, and he was so pleased when Angela told him he picked the right doll.

*   *   *

That winter, Margie gets hospitalized for double pneumonia.

"Is Margie going to be okay? She's so little, and I need to be with her." Angela is on the brink of tears.

"Oh, Angela. Your sister will be fine. The doctors and nurses are taking care of her. You don't need to worry." Mrs. Wilson hugs Angela, trying to replace her fears with reassurance.

"But I need to see her. She shouldn't be alone."

"Margie's not alone, Honey. Lots of people are there taking care of her."

"They aren't her family, and she doesn't know them. What if she's scared?"

"Why don't we go visit tomorrow, and you can see for yourself that she is fine?"

"Okay. I know Margie wants me to be with her."

It shocks Angela to see Margie standing in a crib when they visit her in the hospital. She is indignant.

They're treating Margie as if she were a baby! Don't they know she is six years old?

But her sister looks so small and frail standing there, Angela wants to cradle her in her arms. Margie's recovery and return to the Wilsons' house relieve Angela. Now she can resume looking after her little sister.

Life with the Wilsons continues to be safe, healthy, and happy. Angela enjoys being with her father and siblings and having a natural family, but the Wilson family is home to her. The child adores them, can be carefree because no one criticizes her, and the adults take responsibility for her and Margie. Angela can stop worrying over what will happen next and be a child again. But, what should be and what is are not always the same.

In April, around one year after the girls arrived, the Wilsons look nervous when bringing Margie and Angela into the living room.

"What's wrong?" Angela asks.

"Mommy is ill and can't take care of you anymore," Joe swallows hard.

"But where will we go?" Angela's stomach churns, and her heart is racing.

Please, God! Don't let us go to the Children's Center again!

"You are going to a new foster home." Lena struggles to say the words.

"We love you both very much." Joe keeps clearing his throat.

"And we hate to see you go, but we have no choice." Lena is now crying.

"Don't cry. Margie and I will be fine. Don't worry. But are you going to be okay? What's wrong with you?"

"I'll be fine. The doctors will help me. I'm just not strong enough to take care of you anymore." Lena hugs the girls and cries again.

"But what if I helped? You won't have to work. I'll take care of Margie."

"No, you need an adult taking care of you." Now Lena is wailing.

"You'll be leaving tomorrow, but I want you to know that if you ever need something, you call me. I'll always be here for you." Joe's eyes fill with tears. The four of them hug each other.

Because most of the family will be at work or school in the morning when the girls will leave, they say their goodbyes that night. Everyone is crying. Jane hugs Angela with a fierceness that lets her know she does not want her to go. The Carcieri girls are the only foster children the Wilsons ever have.

*   *   *

Regardless of the outcome and the pain it caused, it was a special blessing for Angela to have joined the Wilson family, even if only for a short while. Mr. Wilson was the first angel she encountered in her life—the kind she learned are on earth to help those in need on God's behalf.

Angela believes the Wilsons had saved her by proving genuine, kind, and good people exist, which gave her hope. They introduced her to a personal God, and her faith was nourished and grew in their care, providing a foundation that will last a lifetime. These admirable people helped her to believe she was loveable. They showed her what a family should be and what a happy life is. Joe and Lena enabled Angela to be a child and experience safety. She grew while in their care, developing confidence, improved self-esteem, and assertiveness because they loved her. Angela will be forever grateful for Joe, Lena, their children, and the blessing it was to live with them. Her next foster home will convince Angela how blessed she was to live with the Wilsons. She will not be safe again for years.

* * *

Seven-year-old Angela is trying to be brave, but she cannot fall asleep. Her mind is racing.

Where are they taking us? What if the new people are mean and hit us as Ruth did? If Mrs. Wilson cannot take care of us, how can she take care of her other children? Ray is only eight years old! If we were their real children, they wouldn't get rid of us. What if something is wrong with me? Then nobody will want me for long. Is it my fault Margie has to leave the Wilsons because we're sisters? Worst, what if the Wilsons never loved us?

Before crying herself to sleep that night because she does not want to leave her home and the family she loves, Angela vows never to trust anyone again.

7

THE SCHNEIDERS

Paul and Dorothy Schneider, who live only two miles from the Wilsons, are Angela and Margie's new foster parents. Unlike the Wilsons, they have been doing foster care for many years as a business. They have three children of their own: a son, John, who is serving in the military; a fifteen-year-old daughter, Denise; and a nine-year-old-son, Jimmy. Their last foster children left a week ago, and the Carcieri girls are their replacements.

Right away, Angela knows this home will differ from the Wilsons'. Mrs. Schneider does not even put on a warm front for the social worker. After a simple, expressionless "Hi," she focuses on business and addresses the girls with a command. "Go to your bedroom, first door on the right from the hallway, and put your clothes in the bureau. Make sure you put everything away and put your trash bags in the pantry off the kitchen. Then come back here." Angela felt as if she should salute her.

When they finish, the girls discover their social worker has left without telling them. Mrs. Schneider rattles off a list of house rules to follow. She does not show any interest in her new foster children or try to get acquainted. Then she sends them to play in the yard. Angela has questions, but her instincts tell her not to ask.

At dinner that night, the family sits at the kitchen table, but Mrs. Schneider seats Angela and Margie in a far corner of the dining room. From their folding card table, they cannot see the rest of the family or the food they are eating, nor are they included in the conversation. The girls' dinner is a small dish of applesauce and one slice of white bread each. For the rest of their stay with the Schneiders, Angela and Margie have their meals alone at that folding table. One peanut butter and jelly sandwich is another typical dinner for them, and they never receive snacks. The food tastes good but is not nourishing enough to be a steady diet. A meal containing meat, poultry, fish, fruit, vegetables, or hot food is rare. One of Mrs. Schneider's rules is that the sisters may not access the cupboards or refrigerator. They are often hungry.

When the girls go for their biweekly visits to Luigi's apartment, Angela always overeats, as if she were a bear storing up for hibernation. The child knows it will be another two weeks before she will have a nutritious, hot meal to squelch the hunger pangs that have become too familiar. Because the Schneiders are overweight, and Angela can smell the meat and other foods cooking at their house, she knows they eat better than she and Margie. Those old feelings Angela experienced at the Children's Center are returning—self-doubt, not belonging, and being inferior.

Another rule at this foster home is that Angela and Margie are not to leave their bed in the morning until Mrs. Schneider comes to get them, except to go to the bathroom. As most young children do, they awaken around six a.m. The Schneiders do not arise until at least seven a.m., and even later on weekends. To entertain themselves for the hour or more between the time they awaken and when they may get up, the sisters talk and play in the bed, pretending to be teachers and such.

One morning, around a week after Angela and Margie arrived at their new house, they are in bed playing and giggling. Mrs. Schneider bursts through their bedroom door and slaps them across the face several times, yelling at them to stop making any noise, or she will give them a beating. The girls lie there and cry into their pillows to muffle the sound. Afterward, they whisper in the mornings as soft as they can manage. But it will not be the last time Mrs. Schneider hits them, and she does not use only her hands.

Even though the parish school is close by, Angela and Margie cannot finish the last couple of months of the school year there. Mrs. Schneider finds it too bothersome to get the girls back and forth. So, she has the social worker enroll the sisters in the nearby public school, where they can walk back and forth on their own. Their stomachs are in knots going into a new school by themselves. The sisters hold hands and gather strength from each other.

New kids at school are always a novelty, more so when they arrive late in the school year, so Angela gets her peers' attention. In the beginning, her classmates talk to her, invite her into their games at recess, and she makes a few friends. One girl, a year older and a grade ahead of Angela, lives a few houses from the Schneiders, and they walk back and forth to school together with Margie. Angela assumes her new friend is wealthy because she always has candy and money. Once in a while, her friend gives her a nickel to buy treats. Angela buys candy in boxes or bags containing several pieces. She always presents Margie with half the candy, then rations the rest, allowing herself only one or two pieces per day so they will last.

When Angela's friend discovers she and Margie are state wards, she tells the other children at school, stops walking with the girls, and shares no more candy. The Carcieri sisters learn people dislike foster children. Their classmates stop playing with them, others laugh at them and call them "state kids" as if they were freaks or had a horrible, contagious disease. A few of her peers tell Angela their mothers told them to stay away from her and said, "State kids are nothing but trouble." Angela decides it best not to make any more friends.

The Schneiders live in the rented first-floor flat of a two-story tenement house. The occupants of the second floor have children, too, so when Mrs. Schneider banishes the girls to the yard, they do not mind. Jimmy, the Schneiders' nine-year-old, and the three children from upstairs play games together in the yard. Angela thinks they might not know she and Margie are foster children. While the child has not bonded to Jimmy or the second-floor tenants, being able to be carefree when they play together often helps Angela to bear her life. Sometimes, she even forgets her misery while they are together.

*   *   *

Although her new foster family does not go to church, Angela can still make her First Communion in May. The ceremony is at the Wilsons' church because she had taken the preparation classes there. A Sister from the parish school calls Angela's social worker. The woman then instructs Mrs. Schneider to send Angela to finish the preparations and make her First Communion.

No one will attend the ceremony for her, but it does not surprise her. Angela invites Luigi to the event, but he says he cannot go. She does not expect the Schneiders to attend, and they will not let Margie go with her. Angela wears a borrowed, white veil and white-lace dress that is too large for her scrawny, malnourished body and goes to her First Communion alone in the taxicab Mrs. Schneider has summoned.

When she receives the Eucharist for the first time, Angela is in awe of the miracle that has taken place. She believes God's spirit now lives in her, and, as a result, others will know she is somebody. Angela wants to make God proud.

At the end of the service, the children move in step, forming a procession of white dresses and suits inching their way up the center aisle. As they walk, Angela notices people taking pictures and waving at their children. Everyone has someone there, except her. She is just as starved for affection and attention as she is for food, but she refuses to be glum on such a special day.

As Angela nears the back of the church, she hears someone call her name. She looks up to see the entire Wilson family standing at the rear of the church, smiling and waving. The child thinks her heart will burst with joy! Angela so wants to run into their arms, but the nuns told the children not to break rank until they reach the parish hall next door, where a special Communion Breakfast in their honor is awaiting them. So the obedient Angela stays in line. Mr. Wilson calls out,

"We'll meet you next door at breakfast." Angela can barely contain her excitement when she nods with a broad smile on her face. When she is a few yards from the parish hall, Denise, the Schneiders' fifteen-year-old daughter, pulls Angela out of the line.

"Come on."

"But I have to go to the Communion Breakfast." The panic surges through her body.

"No, Mom said I have to bring you home."

"Please, can I just tell the Wilsons that I can't go to breakfast? They're waiting for me." Angela's heart is racing as she pleads with her foster sister.

"No, we have to leave now."

Angela obeys, but the happiness and excitement she had just a few moments ago turn into despair. She does not even have the energy for anger. The turn of events deflates and defeats her.

When they arrive at the house, they have no celebration. Mrs. Schneider orders Angela to change her clothes and go outside as if it were just an ordinary day.

Don't they know how important today is? Can't they see I am different now, that I am holier because Christ has transformed me?

That innocent, seven-year-old girl thinks the change in her is visible, and she expects people to treat her well. The Schneiders wipe that notion right out of her head.

The Wilsons occupy Angela's thoughts, and she aches to see them.

Why don't they ever visit Margie and me? Did they forget us? Maybe Mrs. Schneider or the state won't let them.

The girl knows she cannot ask Mrs. Schneider to take her to see them. Angela also knows she cannot ask the woman for any favors, and she never even tries. So, when Angela sees her father, she begs him to take her to visit her former family. After multiple episodes of pleading, Luigi agrees and stops at the Wilsons' house for a brief, unannounced visit on their way to his apartment.

When Mrs. Wilson answers the door, she shrieks in delight and gives Angela and Margie big hugs. Jane, who is ironing, lifts Angela right over the top of the ironing board and squeezes her in a bear hug.

"Oh, my goodness! You got so thin!"

Since they are visiting on a Saturday, most of the family are home. Their joy in seeing the girls is genuine and undeniable. For Angela, this reaffirms their love for her, and she is ecstatic. She explains to the family why she could not meet them after her First Communion and hopes they were not angry at her. Angela tells them how much it meant for them to attend her ceremony, and she thanks them.

When Luigi says they must leave, he promises the Wilsons he will bring his daughters to visit again, but he never does.

I hope they don't wait for Luigi, too.

While that visit gives Angela an emotional boost, it makes it more challenging to be with the Schneiders.

School is Angela's refuge. She immerses herself in her work, and the unpleasantries of her life fade away for a while. In her new public school, the second graders are now covering lessons she had learned in first grade at the parish school.

Her teacher has given her more advanced work to keep her interested. Angela aces everything assigned. At the end of the school year, her teacher recommends the child to skip the third grade and advance to the fourth. But Luigi believes it will hamper his daughter, so it does not happen. He is unaware, but Luigi does Angela a big favor by refusing to let her skip a grade. Third grade ends up being a blessing; she meets another angel, Miss. Lynch.

* * *

Miss. Lynch is Angela's third-grade teacher. She is a young, lovely woman who treats her pupils with kindness. Even better, Miss. Lynch is an excellent teacher who makes learning fun. Back then, girls always wore dresses to school. Although the state gives Mrs. Schneider a clothing allowance for the children (which, in fairness to her foster mother, is inadequate), the girls present as ragamuffins, wearing wrinkled and stained, second-hand, ill-fitting clothes. Angela has only three school dresses she rotates.

On the day the school has scheduled the class pictures, Angela wears one of her old, raggedy dresses. The child is aware of her shabby appearance, adding to her self-consciousness and discomfort. A group of mean, female classmates tells Angela she cannot get her picture taken because she is wearing an ugly, old dress, causing her to cry. Miss. Lynch scolds the girls, puts her arm around Angela, and tells her not only can she get her photo taken, but she will be the first one in line. Angela cannot explain to Miss. Lynch that her tears are not because she wants her picture taken. The girl is crying because of embarrassment and shame. Angela wishes she were invisible.

On the last day of school before Christmas break, Miss. Lynch asks Angela to wait in class for a minute. When her classmates leave the room, her teacher hands Angela a Christmas present. She tells her student Santa Claus left the package at her house by mistake, and Angela should wait until Christmas to open it. Miss. Lynch asks Angela not to discuss the gift with her classmates.

"This will be our secret."

The eight-year-old child stopped believing in Santa the year prior, so she knows the present is from Miss. Lynch. When she comes home from school with the package, Mrs. Schneider asks where she got it. Angela tells her.

"Why in the world did she do that?"

Angela did not bother to respond.

On Christmas morning, the present from Miss. Lynch is the only gift under the Schneiders' tree with Angela's name on it. She feels terrible because Margie has nothing under the tree, so she says she wants to bring her unopened gift to her father's house. She knows her father will have something for Margie, too.

When Angela uncovers the box from Miss. Lynch at her father's apartment, it contains a lovely blue dress with tiny flowers strewn over it and has a lace collar. Miss. Lynch's generosity overwhelms Angela, who cries when she sees the dress. The excited girl finds it the most beautiful thing she has ever seen, and she cannot wait to show it to those mean girls at school. Angela runs to the shared bathroom and tries on her present. It looks as if they tailored it for her. The child never had a dress fit so well, and it makes her look less skeletal. As she walks the public hallway to return to Luigi's apartment, she hopes the neighbors see her. The thrilled little girl wears her lovely new dress the entire day, feeling as if she is a princess.

That winter, the Schneiders' older son, John, comes home on leave from the military. He had been overseas and, two years before, had fought in the Korean War. When John is home, Mr. Schneider finds his voice and talks more to John during his leave than he's uttered in the several months since the Carcieri girls arrived. Mr. Schneider does not speak to the girls. Angela can count on one hand the words he has ever directed at her, and he never looks at her or Margie. It feels as if they do not even exist to him.

John is so unlike the rest of his family. A soft-spoken, neat, clean, and polite man, he stands out as a bright light. John shakes Angela's and Margie's hands.

"So nice to meet you," he says. The man treats the girls as if they were real people. John inquires into their school activities and behaves as if they matter. The family has a big celebratory dinner that night at the kitchen table, and the food smells wonderful.

While eating their corn flakes cereal for dinner, the sisters can hear the conversation in the kitchen.

"Why aren't Angela and Margie at the table with us?" John's tone is edgy.

"Oh, they're fine; don't worry about them."

"They're little kids who should eat with the family, not in another room by themselves."

"The girls enjoy it this way. Besides, we don't have enough room."

Mrs. Schneider changes the conversation, and John stops arguing as if resigned to his words having no impact. Regardless, within a few minutes, John comes into the dining room with a plate of sliced turkey and gives it to Angela and Margie, who devour it. For the first and only time in the Schneider house, they each get a piece of chocolate cake, courtesy of John, another of Angela's angels. They consume every crumb, and Angela wants to lick the plate. John is not home during dinner for the rest of his brief leave, which disappoints the girls. He has a girlfriend and spends most of his time at her house. Whenever John is home, he smiles at Angela and Margie, speaks to them, and treats them well.

One evening during John's leave, Angela awakens around 11:00 p.m., and gets out of bed to use the bathroom. When the girl is walking toward the darkened dining room, she sees the television light flickering and hears the turned-low volume.

As Angela enters the dining room, John is lying atop his girl-friend on the carpeted floor in front of the television. They are both clothed, but he jumps up, is blushing, and fidgeting. Angela figures he and his girlfriend had been kissing, just as Jane did with her boyfriend. She says hello and continues to the bathroom. When Angela reenters the dining room, no one speaks, so she goes back to her bed.

After that, John avoids Angela and has no eye contact with her. John's change confuses Angela, and she obsesses over what she might have done wrong. Still, the child hates to see John go when his military leave ends. He says goodbye, but Angela never sees him again. The child wishes she told him she appreciated his kindness and was sorry if she upset him.

Mrs. Schneider acts as if she wishes the girls were not there. The woman tells them to go outside whenever the weather permits. Every weekend, rain or shine, she sends Angela and Margie to the local movie theater to watch a double feature on their own. Their foster mother gives no consideration to which movies are playing, nor is she concerned for their safety. For the first eight months they attend the theater, the sisters are only ages six and seven. Angela experiences the dangers first hand.

One day, on their way to the movies around half a mile away, a dilapidated, old, green automobile pulls up to the curb alongside the girls. The gray-haired, heavy-set man driving the car rolls down his window and asks where the sisters are going. Angela has an immediate and intense sense of foreboding. The hair on her arms stands at attention. She knows this man and the grubby-looking woman in the passenger seat are bad people. When it happens, Angela does not realize how she knows, but she has no doubt. Before her sister can stop her, Margie tells the stranger where they are going.

"Are you girls alone?" He does not take his beady eyes off the girls, and even his voice sounds creepy.

"Yes," Margie responds. Angela tells her not to talk to the man.

"Come on; we'll give you a ride."

"Okay." Margie heads toward his car, but Angela grabs her sister's arm and pulls her back where she was.

"No, thank you." Angela pulls Margie along with her. The man persists and tries to lure the girls into the car. Angela holds onto Margie, stays as near the buildings and far from the street as possible, keeps walking, and refuses to look at or respond to the man. The man and woman watch the girls for a few seconds, then drive away.

Angela thanks God they are on a busy street. Otherwise, she believes the couple could have kidnapped them.

Great! The people who should want us, don't, and the people who should not want us, do!

As unattended little girls, the sisters are easy prey to another danger: bullies. A boy who is much taller than they and around eleven years old, goes to the same theater most weekends. For no known reason, he punches Angela in the stomach as they are walking home. She tells him to stop, but he laughs and runs away. The bullying happens every week, and Angela dreads the walk back to the house. She tries to outsmart the boy by waiting a while before exiting the theater, but he remains outside until they come out. She attempts to leave before the movie is over, but he follows them out of the theater. It never enters her mind to fight back or defend herself. The fight has gone out of Angela, who, again, can no longer experience anger.

The boy continues to hurt Angela for several weeks, with a few reprieves. One day, he punches both Angela and Margie, and a man sees it happen. He runs over and grabs the boy by the neck, then scolds him.

"What do you think you're doing, Punk? You think you're a tough guy because you can beat on little girls? Maybe you want a taste of your own medicine. You want to see how it feels to get beaten up by someone bigger and older than you?"

"Leave me alone. I didn't do anything to them!"

"If you ever touch them again, I will call the police, and you'll go to jail. Do you hear me?"

"Yeah, let me go!"

"I will be watching you. Now get out of here."

The boy runs away, and that ends the bullying. The man asks the girls if they are okay. Angela is most grateful, and she thanks the man for his kindness.

Another angel!

On a positive note, through her weekly trips to the movie theater, Angela falls in love with film. She can lose herself, without fear or worry, in a whole new world full of laughter, love, excitement, and drama playing out on the enormous screen in front of her. The technicolor pictures make the stories so much more vivid than the black and white television at home. Angela immerses herself in the story plots, music, and dancing. These excursions to the movies are a pure escape for the little girl for a few hours a week, and she loves them. She even enjoys the newsreels preceding the main features.

The news story most piquing Angela's interest is a report of the police arresting Ms. Rosa Parks for disobeying the segregated seating law in her state. She refused to give her bus seat to a white person. Even seven-year-old Angela knows discrimination based on race is nonsensical. The child keeps repeating to herself that it's not fair, and the injustice eats away at her. Angela admires Ms. Rosa Parks' bravery, and it leaves a lasting impression on her. The little girl wishes she could have courage like that instead of cowering in fear most of the time.

Besides the movies, another enjoyable pastime for Angela is watching television programs after school every weekday with Margie and Jimmy Schneider. While sitting cross-legged on the dining room floor, they watch *Salty Brine's Shack* (a locally broadcast children's show), *The Howdy Doody Show,* and *The Mickey Mouse Club.* Angela dreams that one day she can be a

Mouseketeer just like the famous Annette Funicello, and she hopes for a dog just like Salty Brine's handsome collie, Jeff. She still thinks of Fluffy and misses him.

* * *

As the adult Angela reassesses those days with the Schneiders, it strikes her that even in the worst of times, there were moments of fun, laughter, and hope. Still, the unpleasant realities of life with Mrs. Schneider were more prevalent for the little girl.

* * *

Besides exposing the children to danger, not providing adequate nourishment, abusing them, and failing to give Angela and Margie any attention or affection, Mrs. Schneider neglects their hygiene. They have head-lice that go untreated except for a weekly or bi-weekly fine-tooth combing. Mrs. Schneider has an enormous roll of thick, white paper, from which she cuts a large enough piece to cover the kitchen table. Then she uses a fine-tooth comb to remove the lice. The woman squishes the bugs with the nail of her thumb when they hit the paper.

The lice infestation is so severe that a few bugs fall onto her desk at school when Angela scratches her head. She squashes them, copying Mrs. Schneider, and hopes none of her classmates will notice. The itching never stops.

Sometimes, their foster mother gets irritated at having to manage the lice problem. If the girls squirm or dare to say, "*Ow*" when she pulls their hair while combing, Mrs. Schneider smacks them in the head with her hand or whatever she is holding. Then, with a contorted face, she shouts at them.

"Shut up and stop moving, damn it!" Then she combs even rougher.

Luigi continues to bring his children to visit his parents, and Angela is getting to know them. Even at her young age,

Angela knows her grandmother, Nonna, is the family boss. Everyone obeys her, even Nonno, and when she talks, people listen. She is a no-nonsense person, whom Angela thinks is always judging her. Nonna, also, is an immaculate housekeeper, and Angela admires her home. It smells clean, looks neat, and her grandmother decorates with style and sophistication. The house is full of elegant furniture that looks unused, and the handsome, dark wood pieces gleam. Nonna displays the expensive china and crystal Angela loves in a glass-fronted, antique china cabinet. The girl could gaze at it for hours, but she dares not ask permission to enter the dining room, which looks as if a red velvet rope should be across the entrance.

At every visit, Nonna wears an apron and is preparing Italian food in the pantry. The pantry is open to the kitchen, enabling Nonna to visit while she is cooking and wielding a big wooden spoon. Angela knows when her father says something Nonna doesn't approve of because she bops him with the spoon. Luigi laughs when this happens. Angela interprets their exchange as a funny game between the pair.

A huge pot of homemade tomato sauce, meatballs, sausages, and braciole is simmering on the stove. The sauce fills the house with the most appealing aromas, reminding her of the Santoros' kitchen. But unlike Mrs. Santoro, Nonna does not offer the children any food. The sauce is for Sunday dinner, not today. Angela has never eaten a meal at her grandparents' house.

In contrast to her husband, Nonna is talkative and asks her grandchildren questions. Her nickname for Angela is "Meow-Meow." Worried that something is wrong with her, Angela is still timid and does not speak to people with whom she is uncomfortable. When she has to answer a question, her voice is as soft as a whisper, and Nonna Carcieri says she sounds like a kitten meowing; hence, the nickname. Nonna does it in a friendly tone and means no harm, but self-conscious Angela believes she is being criticized and ridiculed.

Except for Nonno and Auntie Concetta, Angela senses no warmth from her father's family, and being with them is the same as visiting strangers. She wonders if her father experienced the same coldness when he was a child. The children sit and only speak when the adults ask them a question. They never play together at their grandparents' house and seldom enjoy themselves there.

Regardless, she is content at Luigi's apartment, where the children are accepted and have fun. Angela's visits with Luigi are even more important to her since coming to the Schneider house. They are a lifeline, giving her hope that her life will be better someday.

Sometimes on those visits, Angela's and Margie's bodies are so dirty that Alice puts them in the bathtub and scrubs them with a brush. After this happens a few times, Alice and Luigi question the girls on their life with the Schneiders. Angela and Margie, whose fear kept them from reporting what was happening, tell the truth when asked outright, but only respond to specific questions. They give no unsolicited information, so Luigi does not know everything Mrs. Schneider does to them. After answering the questions, Angela bursts into tears.

"Don't tell Mrs. Schneider! She'll know I told! Please, she can't know I told."

"Don't worry," Luigi says. "Mrs. Schneider won't know you told us. I'll take care of everything."

"You promise you won't tell her?"

"I promise."

Despite everything, Luigi brings his children back to the Schneider house that same evening and leaves them there.

When the school year ends a few months later, Mrs. Schneider calls Margie and Angela into the kitchen.

"You're both moving to a new foster home. The two girls who lived here before want to return. We are fond of them, and we don't have enough room to keep you, too, so you'll be leaving in the morning."

"Where will we be going?"

"They didn't tell me. You'll find out tomorrow."

The news thrills Angela, but it stings, too, because again the message is: others are better and more desirable. Although she hates being with the Schneiders, it hurts to be unwanted.

8

THE LUNDGRENS

Angela's next foster home is her fourth placement in the three years since her mother died. By now, she has stopped expecting or hoping because her life is so unpredictable. From one day to the next, she does not know where or with whom she will live, and whether they will be decent people. The last thing she needs is any more disappointment. Angela knows having no expectations and focusing on coping with whatever she has to face is best. But, Angela is less fearful of going to this new house because her older sister, Teresa, has been living there for the past year. Angela breathes easier, knowing Teresa will look out for her and Margie.

Alfred and Irene Lundgren are a nice enough couple in their early fifties. They have three adult children living with their own families, and a twelve-year-old son, Ted, who is still at home. Besides Teresa and Ted, Irene's elderly, bed-ridden mother and Angela's brother, Gino, live with them. Gino arrived a few months earlier than Angela.

Their two-story cottage in a rundown neighborhood needs maintenance and repair. While the interior is clean and homey, it looks worn and dated. Angela and Margie will share Teresa's large bedroom on the second floor, and Ted and Gino share a smaller bedroom on the same level. More bedrooms are on the first floor, along with the family room, kitchen, and a large parlor full of overstuffed, old-fashioned furniture they never use.

The family room is where everyone spends their time. While the household is enjoying television programs, such as *Lassie, Gunsmoke,* and The *Ed Sullivan Show*, Mrs. Lundgren tatts doilies, swinging her foot at the ankle the entire time, as if in rhythm to a silent melody playing in her head. Angela finds the tatting and foot-swinging comforting. Those evenings are peaceful, and though Mr. and Mrs. Lungren do not show the warmth or affection that the child received from the Wilsons, Angela finds their home pleasant.

A few weeks after the girls arrive at the Lundgrens', Mrs. Schneider drops by to deliver a few articles of clothing the girls had forgotten. Although Angela and Margie dislike Mrs. Schneider, they run up the driveway towards her, shouting, "Mommy, Mommy," and hug her. Mrs. Schneider does not return their embrace, but she smiles. By appearances, Angela and Margie miss and care for the woman who neglected and abused them. That is not true. But the girls do not force their behavior or pretend; it is intuitive and automatic. They had learned early on: life is better if those in power are fond of you, so you do everything possible to please them and gain their favor. Otherwise, unpleasant things happen.

Because they arrived at this foster home in the summer, the girls spend a majority of their time playing in the back-yard or on the large, screened front porch. Angela whiles away many hours on that porch, watching the activities in the neighborhood and creating elaborate, imaginary scenarios for the lives of the passersby. The man up the street who wears a suit, comes and goes at different hours, and whose eyes dart everywhere must be a spy or an undercover agent. The teenage girl next door, who never smiles, is planning to run away with her boyfriend because her parents hate him and refuse to allow her to see him.

Angela enjoys fantasizing about a stunning blonde girl around one year older than she. The girl lives on the street that runs perpendicular to the Lundgrens' front porch, so Angela has a birdseye view of the happenings there. The girl wears fashionable outfits, and an average-looking blonde friend always accompanies her. Angela pretends that the girl is a princess from a foreign country, hiding out here for protection from her father's enemies, and her constant companion is her servant. In Angela's fantasies, the princess's parents adore and dote on their daughter, and give her everything she wants. Angela says hello to the princess one day, hoping they can be friends, but the girl does not respond.

Such fantasies help Angela escape the realities of her own life. While she is no longer suffering abuse, has regular meals and good hygiene, the Lundgrens neglect her emotional needs. While they are attentive, warm, and affectionate toward Ted, they show no interest in the girls, as if their wards were mere fixtures instead of feeling human beings. Mr. Lundgren, like Mr. Schneider, never speaks to the girls and is a silent and withdrawn man, but Angela realizes this placement is much better than the Children's Center and the Schneiders' house. She no longer has to live in fear of her next beating, contend with head lice, or cope with frequent hunger pangs.

Sometimes, Angela helps Ted with his paper route. He is friendly towards her, and they talk and laugh while working. Although Ted ignores the girls when they are home, he shows interest in Angela while they deliver newspapers.

"So where did you live before you came, here?"

"At another foster home, but it wasn't very nice."

"Why can't you live with your parents?"

Angela informs Ted of her mother's death and describes her other placements.

"What place was the worst?"

"The Children's Center. It's an orphanage and the first place we went. It was awful there, and I hated it."

"Why?"

"Because one housemother was mean, and other things weren't nice."

"What did she do?"

"I don't want to talk about it. I just hated it and hope I never have to go back there again."

Ted tries to find out more details, but Angela won't answer. She wonders why he was so interested in the Center.

One day in late summer, one of Angela's half-sisters, Laurie, comes to visit with her boyfriend. It is the first time Angela has encountered any of those older siblings since they moved out of their house three years prior. Angela loves seeing her, and they sit on the screened front porch and talk for an hour. They laugh and have fun, and Angela gets the impression that Laurie is just as happy to be with them as they are to be with her. Despite their enjoyment, Laurie disappears for two more years.

In early fall, Mrs. Lundgren's mother dies. Angela never got to know her because the woman was bedridden, so her death is not a loss to the child. Mrs. Lundgren is grieving, though, and Angela is sorry for her. She remembers how awful she felt when Larry died. After her mother's death Mrs. Lundgren, who had been home full-time to take care of her mother, has to return to work. She gets a job working in a factory, and Teresa watches the children after school and prepares dinner for the family. After school, the children sit at the kitchen table doing their homework and, if they have time, they play a game of Sorry.

*　*　*

Mrs. Lundgren, who is religious, enrolls the girls in the local parish school where Ted, Teresa, and Gino have been attending. The older children walk to school, but Angela and Margie ride the bus, so they arrive at their new school alone. Angela ruminates on how her new classmates will assess her and if they will be friendly. Her stomach is in knots on their first day of school but, at least this time, she is starting in September instead of the middle of the school year as in prior school changes. Angela still hates starting new schools every year, not knowing any of her classmates, and being the outsider.

It turns out Gino, two years older than Angela, is in her classroom because he had repeated a grade. Although he is her brother, Angela dislikes him. Gino is insincere, presenting a charming front while plotting something devious. She never knows whether to believe what he is saying. His sister neither trusts him nor is comfortable around him.

Regardless, Angela feels sorry for Gino, assuming he acts out because he wants to be home with his father. She sees how Gino tries to impress his father and get his approval, but he never does. No matter what Gino accomplishes, it does not satisfy Luigi, and he often criticizes his son.

"Dad, I made the baseball team!" Gino had been practicing, and his excitement shows.

"Did you make pitcher?"

"No, they're using the kid who did it last year."

"Then I guess you didn't practice enough." Luigi leaves the room without congratulating his son for making the team.

"Wow, Gino, that's great! Not everyone makes the team. I can't wait to see you play." Angela tries to help Gino with her comment, to no avail.

Besides, Angela sees how disappointed Gino gets with Luigi's repeated broken promises, and he misbehaves every time it happens. Still, something more complicated is going on with her brother. He tries to get Angela in trouble for no logical reason. Daily, their teacher collects missions money for starving children in third world countries. The donating pupils stand beside their desks until the nun comes by with the collection can. After depositing their contribution into the tin, the student goes to the front of the classroom and writes their name on a chart posted on the wall. At the end of the month, the child who has donated the most times will get a prize.

Angela asks Mrs. Lundgren if she may have a few coins for the missions. Her foster mother agrees, telling the child to be sure the money gets donated and not spent. Angela finds Mrs. Lundgren's mistrust of her insulting because spending the money never entered Angela's mind. That night at dinner, the woman questions Angela.

"Did you give the missions money to your teacher today?"

"Yes."

"No, she didn't. I was there, and she didn't give any money when the teacher was collecting it," Gino said.

"Yes, I did! Don't you remember I was standing in class and signed the chart?"

Gino is convincing when he continues to lie, and Mrs. Lundgren believes him.

"I'm disappointed in you, and it's a shame I can't trust you."

"But my name is on the chart. Ask Sister Cecile; she'll tell you." The girl's stomach is in knots, and her heart is racing.

The next evening, after Mrs. Lundgren gets home from work, she says she called Sister Cecile that afternoon. Sister looked at the chart and said Angela's name was not on it. The girl cannot understand how that can be. She remembers being proud as she wrote her name on the sheet of paper. As punishment for lying, Angela cannot watch any television that week. The next day at recess, Angela looks at the posting and can tell someone erased her penciled-in name, which she can still detect. Angela asks Sister Cecile to look at the chart, and her teacher confirms what the girl sees. Angela explains to Sister what happened at home and says she suspects Gino erased her name. Her teacher says she will call Mrs. Lundgren and let her know the truth.

"Why on earth would Gino do that?" Sister asks. Angela is asking herself the same question. She wonders if Gino does such things because he is so sad.

Around this same time, Ted acts weird with Angela. She often finds him staring at her, and when she looks back at him, he averts his eyes. One evening after dinner, she is in the bathroom sitting on the toilet. Without knocking, Ted opens the lockless door and closes it behind him. He is staring at Angela with a twisted smile on his face.

"Why are you in here? Can't you see I'm using it? Get out!" She can't believe what he is doing and feels the blood rush to her face. Ted chuckles and doesn't leave.

"I want to see you."

"You see me every day; get out."

"No, I want to see you there." He is pointing toward the toilet seat.

"You won't see me because I'm not moving until you leave." She tries to cover herself.

"Get out, or I'll tell on you."

"Tell. I'll say that you're lying, and you know my mom will believe me, and you'll be the one in trouble."

Angela refuses to get up from the toilet. At last, Ted peeks out the door into the kitchen, and when he sees no one, he slips out of the bathroom. Angela is beside herself. She slams the bathroom door when she exits the room, and her jaw aches from clenching her teeth. Teresa notices her sister's flushed face, harsh tone, and rough pushing of the chairs as Angela walks by her, so she questions her.

"What's wrong with you? Why are you acting this way?"

Angela hesitates to respond at first, but the words burst out of her.

"I hate Ted!"

"Why? What happened?"

"I was just in the bathroom, and he came in and did not leave. He wanted to see me without clothes, and it scared me.

I can never look at him again after he saw me on the toilet. I hate him!"

"Did he touch you?"

"No!"

"Okay, I'll tell Mrs. Lundgren. He shouldn't be doing that."

When Teresa reports it to Mrs. Lundgren, the woman does not believe her.

"Ted could never do that, and if he was in the bathroom, then Angela must have asked him to come into the room."

From then on, Angela asks Teresa to stand guard whenever she uses the bathroom.

A few weeks later, Angela awakens during the night to find Ted standing over her. He is holding the waistband of her pajama pants away from her and is looking in her pants. Angela jumps out of bed.

"What are you doing? Get out of here!" Ted's boldness shocks the girl. Margie is asleep beside her, and Teresa is sleeping in a bed on the other side of the room. For an unknown reason, Angela does not want to awaken them, so she whispers.

"I'll call Teresa if you don't get out of here." Ted smirks and leaves the room.

Angela avoids Ted now, and her stomach flips whenever he is around, but she tells no one. She knows Mrs. Lundgren will never believe her, and she doesn't want her foster mother to dislike her any more than she does.

In September, the family visits a relative's house on a Sunday evening. Everyone gathers around the television, excited over a singer named Elvis Presley performing on The Ed Sullivan Show. Eight-year-old Angela has never heard of him, but the teenage girls at the house are jumping up and down in excitement. He plays guitar, is handsome, sings in front of his band, and you can tell he is swiveling his hips even when the camera shows him only from the waist up at first.

The studio audience comprises hysterical, teenage girls who are crying, screaming and acting crazy. Angela cannot understand why they are behaving this way. The adults in the room are discussing how scandalous Elvis is during the second part of his performance when they show his full body gyrating. Angela is unimpressed and unaware that she just witnessed a historic event.

* * *

Within a month of starting school, Gino leaves the Lundgrens. He has become too much for them to handle. The boy gets into trouble both at school and at home, and the adults consider him unmanageable. Gino's departure relieves Angela, but she still feels sorry for him. And Gino's misdeeds continue to have adverse effects on his sister. His repeated lies about Angela result in Mrs. Lundgren suspecting the girl. Her foster mother's mistrust leaves Angela vulnerable, and her anxiety rises. If Mrs. Lundgren does not trust her, it puts Angela in jeopardy. Ted lies, too, reinforcing his mother's mistrust of the girl. At least Ted has a reason to lie; he does it protect himself.

One day, Mrs. Lundgren finds a knick-knack broken and hidden under a cushion in the living room.

"Who did this?" Nobody answers.

"I want to know who did this!" Mrs. Lundgren's voice is louder and more stern.

"It wasn't me, but I saw Angela in there the other day." Angela now knows Ted did it.

"Well?" Mrs. Lundgren is glaring at Angela and expecting her to admit she did it.

"No, it wasn't me!" Angela's heart is racing again, and her voice quivers.

For days, Mrs. Lundgren badgers Angela to admit she is lying. Then she threatens the girl with punishment. "If you don't admit that you lied, then you aren't going to the party next week."

This party is special. A classmate lives on a farm, and her family owns horses. She has invited her entire class to her birthday party. Her guests will ride the horses, which Angela has never done. She has been so excited to go to the party and has been counting the days. Still, Angela continues to be honest, saying she did not lie.

Two days before the party, desperate to attend, Angela gives in and admits to breaking something she did not break, and to lying when she did not lie. To her credit, Mrs. Lundgren keeps her word and allows Angela to go to the party, but she metes out another punishment and never trusts the girl again. The woman now thinks of her as a liar and believes nothing Angela says. Later, Teresa asks her sister if she broke the knick-knack, or if she only confessed so she could go to the party. To avoid getting into more trouble, Angela lies again and tells Teresa she broke it.

At school, things continue to go well with Angela's classes, but she is still self-conscious and shy. As a result, she does not have many friends. A few boys tease her and call her "Skinny Minny." To make matters worse, the school belongs to a French parish, so every pupil must take French class every year. Most of the children in Angela's class have been taking French since kindergarten, have French surnames, and do well in French class. Thus, Angela, who has never studied the language before, struggles with it and is not as proficient as her classmates. For the first time since kindergarten, Angela does not rank top of her class. She believes she is inferior and loses confidence in her abilities. Her Italian last name does not help, either. The other students think her name is weird and mispronounce it on purpose. They laugh when they call her the "eye-talian" girl. She is an outcast.

Ted is another worry. Ever since Gino left, he keeps trying to get Angela alone. She is uneasy around him and avoids him as much as she can. One afternoon after school, Teresa is not at the house, so only Ted, Angela, and Margie are present. Ten minutes later, a neighbor friend of Margie's comes to play. They both go to the yard, and Angela follows them.

"Where are you going?" Ted asks.

"Outside to play with Margie."

"No, I'm in charge today. We'll play a game in here."

The obedient Angela goes to get the Sorry game they often play after school.

"No, I have a new game, up in my room."

"Well, go get the game and bring it here." Angela's chest tightens.

"What? Are you afraid that I'll play better than you? Come on; it'll be fun."

Against her better judgment, Angela follows Ted up to his room. When he closes the door, Angela's muscles contract, and her body is on hyper-alert. Ted pushes her onto the bed.

"I'm going to show you how to make babies." His tone is matter-of-fact.

"What do you mean?" Angela's heart is now racing, and she finds it more difficult to breathe. The child has no clue how to make babies, but fear is consuming her. Ted is kissing her, and although Angela has not reached puberty, he is rubbing her undeveloped chest and putting his hands all over her.

"Stop it! I don't want to make babies." She is now in a full panic.

"You're too young; you can't have a baby." Ted laughs, but Angela's wrists hurt where he is retraining her.

"I don't want to play this game." Angela is pleading for him to stop and feels as if she is suffocating. Ted does not stop and is grinding his genitals against her. He pulls off her clothes and says,

"Don't worry; you'll love it."

Her stomach flips, and Angela squeezes her eyes shut as tight as she can, the same way as she does whenever she sees something frightening on TV or at the movies. The child tries to focus on the chirping bird she can hear through the window. She is envious of that free bird who can fly away at whim. Angela is attempting to imagine herself somewhere else. She was successful doing that in the past, when things were unpleasant. But the physicality and pain of the attack jolt her back to the ugly reality of what is happening. Ted is raping her. It hurts, and the child is crying and begging him to please stop. Ted could not care less what Angela wants.

When he finishes with her, Angela runs out of the room to the bathroom where she vomits, then cleans herself. When she sees blood on the washcloth, it terrifies her. Angela worries whether Ted damaged something inside her and whether the bleeding will stop. But the child cannot risk revealing her injury because Ted warns her if she ever tells anyone, she will have to go back to the Children's Center. Angela stuffs a wad of toilet paper inside her panties, then curls into a ball on the bathroom floor, hugging a towel.

* * *

Why didn't I fight? Why didn't I scream? Such thoughts plague the adult Angela when she relives the rape. Many emotions she experienced on the day of the rape return, but now anger is in the mix.

I made a terrible mistake! What was I thinking? I should never have come back here or tried to relive my childhood. She runs from the beach to the safety of her car, pounds the steering wheel, and screams profanities at Ted. She is angry at herself for not fighting as a child and for making the mistake of revisiting her childhood now.

But once the flood of emotions and her tirade against Ted and herself exhaust her, she is calm enough to reason and be rational again. Angela recognizes she, as an eight-year-old submissive child, who was full of fear and lacked any sense of self-worth, did not have the wherewithal to reason and act like the adult she is today. The woman can now sympathize with the child she was, and she wishes the young girl could have had sympathy for herself. *But I can't do this anymore. I've had enough. I should have left the past buried.* Angela starts the ignition and drives toward the hotel to collect her suitcase and head home.

Despite her best efforts, Angela cannot get a flight home until the next morning. She has a restless night and, for the first time in decades, has a nightmare of the rape. It convinces her the decision to reassess her childhood was an error in judgment. During her first week back home, she cannot stop ruminating on her childhood and cannot sleep. She recognizes she needs help and meets with a psychologist.

"You were on the right track in deciding to reprocess your trauma. That is the best method we have to treat Post Traumatic Stress symptoms such as your nightmares."

"But it was awful. It caused my nightmares to return."

"The nightmares will only be temporary. The more we reprocess, the more they will fade until the trauma stops haunting you. We have a specific process we use. I think you overwhelmed yourself by reviewing the entire assault at once. Therapy will be different. We will review pieces at a time, and I will help by engaging each of your senses, to make the scene as vivid as possible."

"I don't know, Doctor. It sounds risky."

"The treatment is difficult, but it works. We will go at your pace, and you will be in total control. Let me explain it in detail, and then you can decide."

After getting her questions answered, and upon the doctor's advice, Angela agrees to do the therapy sessions, with the doctor's assurance that Angela will be in control. She brings the psychologist up to speed, and, after a few weeks in therapy, they continue where she left off that day at the beach and reprocess the trauma the proper way.

*   *   *

Angela, as a child, has no sympathy for herself following the rape. Instead, she faces shame and a sense of worthlessness. Unable to look anyone in the eye that evening, the child says she is ill and pretends to read a book, staying with the adults. Under the guise of fear over being sick, Angela convinces Teresa to go upstairs and stay with her at bedtime.

In response to losing control over even her own body, her anxiety and impulsivity increase, and she experiences an ultimate sense of powerlessness. Angela has nightmares and starts wetting the bed, which incites Mrs. Lundgren's anger. She scolds the child, embarrassing her. Besides, Angela is admonishing herself for not listening to her instincts and going upstairs with Ted. She lives in fear of her attacker and worries someone will discover what happened, causing a return to the Children's Center.

When Angela's school grades slip, and she keeps complaining of stomachaches, Mrs. Lundgren contacts the social worker to tell her something must be wrong with Angela. The social worker takes the girl for a ride and asks her if everything is okay. But Angela, who had seen the woman once, will not confide in her. She trusts nobody and only responds, "Everything is fine." She is too frightened and too ashamed to discuss it. Angela is still only eight years old.

The church is next door to the school, and Angela finds solace going there to pray during the lunch break each day. She eats a bagged lunch at a table in the school basement along with Margie, Teresa, and several other children. Since many children go home for lunch, the period is an hour-long, and she has ample time before afternoon classes start. While her sisters and the others go to play in the schoolyard, Angela goes to pray.

While the girl is in church, the building is empty. Angela loves the peace and solitude, and the safety of being in God's presence. The child likes the slight smell of incense and melting wax from the candles burning in front of a few statues. Angela talks to God just as if she were speaking to a loving father. The little girl thanks God for no longer being alone because He is there to confide in and help her. Angela prays to get a family who will love her and treat her as one of their own. She needs to belong somewhere and craves a sense of safety and connectedness, which comes from living with loving people, such as the Wilsons. The child has stopped hoping to go back with her father. Waiting for Luigi to reunite her family is futile, she realizes, but she continues to wait for evidence of his love for her.

The frightened child asks God to help her avoid getting into any more trouble with Mrs. Lundgren. Angela thanks God for how much better her life is, including no more beatings, a house to live in and having enough to eat. The child asks for forgiveness if she has sinned and for help to be a better person. Every prayer ends by asking God to help every unhappy child in the world.

Sometimes, Angela cries while she talks to God, telling Him she is sorry for what she did with Ted and begs Him to prevent it from happening again. The eight-year-old does not realize she is a victim and not at fault. She believes she is dirty, worthless, and has an ultimate sense of powerless since even her own body no longer belongs to her. The shame makes her want to disappear.

The Carcieri girls continue visiting their father in his two-room apartment. On Thanksgiving Day, he collects his children in the late morning, and they are looking forward to spending the day with him. They do not go to his apartment, though, but to visit his parents. Her grandparents' dining room table, set with china and crystal, looks festive. Angela is wondering if they will have dinner there and gets excited at the possibility.

Instead, they leave and go to visit Auntie Concetta, whose house smells of such delicious food that Angela's stomach growls. Auntie's dining table is fancy, too, set with a lace tablecloth, fine china, crystal, silver, and place settings for fourteen people.

Maybe we will eat here today! But Angela does not dare ask. She finds it curious that Alice is not with them. She wonders if her step-mother is having one of her sick days, which happens often.

Within an hour of arriving, Luigi gets up from his chair. "Okay, kids. Kiss everyone goodbye. We need to get going."

"Bye, Auntie. Happy Thanksgiving."

"Bye, kids. Happy Thanksgiving. Do you want to take a few cookies with you?"

Angela thinks they are going to his apartment now to have Thanksgiving dinner with Alice, who is at home cooking. On their way out the door, though, Auntie Concetta calls to her brother.

"Don't dawdle taking the children home. Dinner is at two-o-clock sharp. If you and Alice are late, we'll start without you." Luigi responds in Italian and hustles the children along.

When Luigi brings the girls back to their foster house, the Lundgrens have finished their Thanksgiving dinner and put away everything. Mrs. Lundgren can't believe Luigi has not fed the girls. She pulls out the leftovers and reheats them, slamming things around, frowning, and telling the sisters they had better clean everything up when they finish eating. Teresa, Angela, and Margie sit by themselves at the kitchen table eating leftover Thanksgiving dinner. Angela thinks they are a burden and unwanted.

Teresa and Margie deserve a better Thanksgiving than this one. It's not fair! Shame on Daddy!

The child realizes, though, she has more than others do. They collected groceries at both the school and church this month for families who, otherwise, could not have a

Thanksgiving meal, not even leftovers. But despite knowing she is blessed, she does not appreciate it right now.

* * *

In December, Angela turns nine years old, but she is like an old lady. She has no energy, longs for the carefree days she had with the Wilsons and wishes she were with them again. From being on guard with Ted, trying to avoid upsetting Mrs. Lundgren, and carrying her secret, Angela has much stress and believes she is alone.

When Angela hears that Mrs. Lundgren's daughter will have a new baby, she has a flashback of Ted's attack and has compassion and pity for the expectant mother. That night, she has another of her nightmares involving Ted. The dreams are always the same. Angela sees Ted's face above her on the bed as he is atop her and holding her down. Angela feels as if she is suffocating. Then his face becomes blurry, and he morphs into a giant, black blob-like monster with no discernible form. The blob keeps growing larger and larger. As it is about to envelop Angela completely and absorb her into itself, her screams awaken her.

In February, the elementary school stages a variety show in the church basement on a Sunday afternoon. For several weeks, Angela has been practicing the song and dance routine she will perform with her fourth-grade classmates. She is excited and informs everyone of her upcoming performance. Angela had joined the church's junior choir in September and loved singing for the congregation every Sunday morning. This choir experience gives her the confidence to be on stage. Two hours before the variety show's start, the Lundgrens leave the house saying they will return in the evening. They take Ted with them and order Teresa to take care of her sisters and feed them leftovers for dinner.

Teresa informs Angela she can no longer take her to the show because she has to watch Margie, so Angela goes alone. Again, Luigi cannot come to see her event, so nobody is there for her. Despite her self-pity, Angela has fun performing and enjoys the show. Still, she wishes Luigi could have been there to clap for her, be proud of her, and take her picture as her classmates' families were doing. The child wonders if she will wait forever for her father to show up for her.

Since the rape, Angela avoids Ted and never allows herself or Margie to be alone with him in the house again. Sometimes, it entails staying outside in freezing temperatures over the winter, but Angela does not mind. She prefers braving the frigid weather to having Ted get ahold of her again.

Over the spring, Angela devotes herself to her schoolwork and brings her grades back to what they were before the rape. The girl seldom laughs or finds joy, trudging through each day without looking forward to something. Angela does not know how she will get through the long summer without schoolwork to occupy her, but she gets through it with God's help. Further, when Teresa takes her and Margie for long walks and brings them with her when she has a babysitting job, it helps Angela. Teresa, who is protective of her sisters, senses Angela needs to be with her. She continues to stand guard at the bathroom door when her sister is using it.

Teresa is much stronger than Angela. She is feisty, fearless, and won't put up with what she thinks is unjust. To Angela, her older sister is much more an adult than a child. Teresa has had several fistfights defending her younger siblings. Sometimes, she even fought boys when Gino got himself into trouble with peers. Those who know her have witnessed her stubborn streak. If Teresa believes she is right, the girl will stand her ground regardless of the consequences. Teresa shows her intense feelings of love and loyalty to her family and gives of herself without reservation to her loved ones. Angela appreciates, admires, and loves her big sister, and does not know how she could fare in this foster home without her. Teresa provides her only sense of security.

The biweekly Saturdays with her father help Angela get through the summer, too. He and Alice take the children to the beach on most visits. They leave in the morning and spend the entire day playing in the ocean Angela so loves, digging in the sand, and having the delicious picnics Alice prepares. She brings a large pan full of meatballs and sausages in her tomato sauce, a dish of eggplant Parmigiano, fresh torpedo rolls to make sandwiches with the meat or eggplant, potato salad, Kool-Aid, and cookies. The food is homemade except for the rolls.

After lunch, Angela hates waiting for the required twenty minutes to elapse before she can return to the water. Luigi and Alice must tire of hearing the children's repeated refrain. "Is it 20 minutes yet?" On those days at the beach, Angela smiles again, plays, and enjoys herself.

While at the beach one day, the family runs into Millie and her children while they are crossing the street. Teresa and Anna hug Millie, and they have a brief and shallow exchange of pleasantries. Millie looks as if she is uncomfortable.

"Who was that?" Angela asks.

"You don't remember her? That's our sister, Millie," Teresa says.

"Oh."

Angela had not seen Millie since their mother's death and had no memories of her before it. Still, not recognizing her sister upsets the little girl.

Before long, September arrives, and Angela enters fifth grade. She knows her classmates and is glad to throw herself into her studies. Ever the good student, Angela has improved her French and is getting top grades again. Too, she resumes her lunchtime visits to church. Although Angela prayed daily throughout the summer, attended mass every Sunday, and experienced God's presence in her life, being alone in the church again is a great comfort. Sure of His love and promise of forgiveness if she is remorseful, Angela continues to tell God everything. She knows her faith gets her through her difficulties and provides the hope she needs.

Thank you, God. You love me, and Jesus died for me, so that must make me worth something!

Angela spends much of her spare time reading, her second favorite thing to do and one rank below being at the ocean. Even on visits to her father's place, Angela will have her nose in a book while her siblings are playing. Reading is a great escape, and when she is perusing a book, she is in control. Angela can choose what, and when she reads, she can stop or continue as long as she likes. This sense of control in at least one part of her life, no matter how small, is vital to this child who is so powerless. Angela loves the smell and texture of books and even enjoys turning the pages.

That fall, Mrs. Lundgren has surgery and is in the hospital for a week. Angela worries for her and prays she will be okay. While Angela knows Mrs. Lundgren dislikes her, her foster mother is a good woman, and the girl wants her well. Teresa handles the household duties while Mrs. Lundgren is recuperating, and Angela wishes her sister, who just turned fifteen, could be out having fun with her friends. She tries to help Teresa where she can and wishes her older sister had a happier life. She senses Teresa's sadness and can empathize with it.

Two weeks before Christmas, and one week after Angela's tenth birthday, Mrs. Lundgren informs the girls they are leaving for a new foster home the next morning. The woman says she has health issues and cannot take care of the girls anymore. Mrs. Lundgren then gives them each a Christmas present, and they receive their first hug from her. A sense of relief washes over Angela at the news, not because the Lundgrens mistreat her, but because she will be free from worrying over Ted, which has been a constant concern.

Angela wonders why they never get advance notice when they leave a foster home. In every placement, the adults informed her only the day before she was to move. Angela does not enjoy such surprises. She needs time to prepare herself and adjust.

After one final putdown from Mrs. Lundgren, who tells Angela to be a good girl and not lie anymore, she informs the girls they are going to a young couple with no children. The woman is only twenty-nine years old, and her husband is thirty-two. Being with a young couple intrigues Angela. She wonders if they will be more fun and less strict because of their age. Several questions run through her mind.

Will they be kind, or will they be mean and hurt us? Do they want us? Will they give us attention, or will they ignore us? What if they don't feed us enough?

The questions continue to flood her mind, but Angela then remembers to expect or hope for nothing, so she is not disappointed. But when she tells herself that she won't have to be with Ted anymore, her face stretches into a smile. Angela does not say goodbye to Ted or even glance at him. She hopes she never sees his face again but knows he will visit her in her nightmares.

9

THE KOWALSKIS: PART 1

P lacement number five for Angela is with Yvette and Henry Kowalski, a childless, young couple who have been fostering a two-year-old boy, Gary, for a year now. Mrs. Kowalski does not have a job outside the home and is a full-time foster mother. Gary is their first foster child, but Yvette has always wanted to be a mother. She is most fond of babies and toddlers.

"This will be your new street," the social worker says. She turns off the main drag onto a side road populated by three-story tenement houses surrounded by chain-link fences.

"Here we are!" Her voice is too cheery as she parks in front of the three-decker house.

With hesitation, the girls walk the long, black tar driveway to the back door. Angela and Margie are holding hands.

"Hello." Yvette is an attractive woman who greets the three sisters with a big smile.

"This is Gary." The cutest little, blonde-haired toddler peeks from behind the woman and flashes a mischievous grin at the girls. Angela can't help but smile at him. Henry, a carpenter, is away at work. Yvette shows Angela and Margie the bedroom they will share, and she helps them unpack their plastic trash bags and put away their meager belongings. Teresa will share Gary's bedroom.

After everyone settles in, Yvette asks the girls lots of questions, trying to get to know them. Her interest in the girls is novel to Angela, and she likes the attention. Yvette impresses her as a warm and friendly person, and the three sisters become less anxious than they were when they arrived.

"Daddy!" Gary yells. Henry, a tall, slender, and handsome man, has come home from work. Gary runs to him and wraps his arms around the man's legs, then Henry and Yvette greet each other with a hug and kiss. Their new foster father smiles at the girls and welcomes them. Yvette puts dinner on the table, and the six of them eat together, talking, and enjoying themselves. Hope is creeping in, despite Angela's better judgment.

After dinner, the girls help Yvette wrap Christmas presents for her relatives. Yvette asks Angela to wrap two gifts for a party the Kowalskis are attending, telling her one package is for the ladies and one is for the men. When Angela writes Ladies on one tag and Gentlemen on the other, Yvette laughs. Angela experiences the familiar fluttering in her chest and the flip-flopping of her stomach.

"What's wrong?" Angela asks.

"Nothing," Yvette responds.

She continues to laugh, but Angela cannot figure out why. Because she is so sensitive, the girl wonders if she has done something wrong, making her uneasy. It never dawned on the child who personalized everything, that Yvette might have been laughing at the thought of calling her rough brothers gentlemen. But being on guard and hypersensitive to others' feelings and opinions have helped Angela manage her unpredictable life. Living in a new home, she is on hyper-alert, and any perceived sign of disapproval causes anxiety.

With only one more week of school before the Christmas recess, the girls will not return to school until after the new year. Margie and Angela will go to the Kowalskis' local parish school, but they allow Teresa, who is in ninth grade and will graduate middle school in June, to finish the year out at their old school. Angela dreads starting a new school in the middle of the year again, but she pushes it out of her mind so she can enjoy the holidays.

One day during the first week at her new placement, Angela overhears Yvette and Teresa discussing her.

"The social worker told me about Angela."

"What do you mean? She doesn't even know Angela. We only met her when she brought us here."

"She said Mrs. Lundgren told her Angela lies all the time, and she told me not to trust her."

"That's not true. Mrs. Lundgren didn't trust Angela, but she's not a liar. I think Angela lied and said she broke something she didn't because Mrs. Lundgren insisted she was lying and forced her to admit it. Another time, our brother said she lied, but we found out he was the liar."

"Well, I guess I will find out for myself."

The social worker's warning affects Yvette, despite what Teresa told her. She often checks with others to verify what Angela says, which makes the insecure girl more self-conscious. Desperate for approval, Angela does everything she can to show she is a good girl.

On Christmas Eve, the family goes to Yvette's parents' house for their traditional French-Canadian meat pies and homemade baked beans. The Carcieri girls meet Yvette's siblings and their families, and people fill the house with laughter and fun. Angela enjoys watching everyone open their presents during their gift exchange. Since the girls arrived at the Kowalskis' just two weeks prior, Yvette's mother states no one had time to get the sisters a gift. Angela understands and does not take offense, although she wishes she and her sisters had a present, too.

On Christmas morning, the Kowalskis and their new foster children watch Gary dump the contents of his Christmas stocking onto the living room floor, then rip open around a dozen presents. He loves everything and is so cute in his excitement, running around as if he were a wind-up toy. Angela is laughing and enjoying this little guy. Then, Yvette hands each of the girls a wrapped Christmas present from the Kowalskis. Angela opens the package with anticipation and finds a pair of blue jeans inside, the same gift her two sisters get. Blue jeans are not yet in fashion, and Angela believes only farmers and cowboys wear them. She hopes nobody will see her in such attire, then smiles at the Kowalskis when she thanks them. Because she hates the gift, the girl feels guilty. Angela knows they did not have to get her something for Christmas.

Late in the morning, Luigi brings the girls to spend the day with him, Alice and their siblings in his tiny apartment. Each of the Carcieri children gets a few gifts from Luigi and Alice. As is their tradition, their Christmas stockings have a peppermint candy protruding from the top, contain other candy, fruit, and nuts in the body, and a tangerine in the toe. The children always open the stockings first, then rip open their presents. Angela takes her time, trying to make the gift opening last longer. She savors the moments.

Angela finds comfort in their traditions, those involving Christmas activities and food. She loves seeing the familiar, porcelain creche figurines. They were under the tree at the old house when her mama was alive. Imported from Italy, Nonno and Nonna gifted them to her father before she was born.

"Daddy, did you have these when you were little, too?" Angela is holding a lamb from the creche.

"Yes, most of them, but we added pieces over the years. Your grandparents didn't allow me to touch them when I was a kid."

"Is that why you let me touch them?"

"Maybe." Luigi chuckles.

"Can I have the figurines when I grow up and have a family? I love them, and nobody else's are as pretty."

"We'll divide them among you kids when I'm too old to use them. But that won't be for a long time yet. You might not want them by then."

"No, Daddy. I will always want them."

Angela takes out a construction paper Christmas card and hands it to her father.

"Here, Daddy. I made this for you. I'm sorry I didn't have any money to buy you a present."

"Oh, you drew the creche on it. Thank you. It's very nice. And I don't need you to buy me a present. You kids are my present." Angela hugs her father, and he kisses her cheek.

The family shares a delicious meal, then plays card games together around the kitchen table, such as Pokeno and Michigan Rummy, until early evening when Luigi returns them to their foster homes. Angela always hates leaving her family to go back to living as an outsider.

On the first day at their new school, Yvette drives Angela and Margie, showing them how to get there because they will walk to school after today. An adult accompanying them to their new school for a change comforts the girls and makes them less afraid. When Mother Superior introduces Angela to her new teacher and class, she sees her peers' eyes on her, and her stomach churns as she takes her seat. At recess, a few of the girls ask her questions, but no one is friendly. Most of her classmates have been together since kindergarten, and Angela is just a stranger who is intruding.

At their new school, Margie and Angela sit together in the lunchroom and are too shy to start conversations with the other children. After several weeks, though, the other children engage more, and Angela makes friends among the less popular kids. Sometimes, she even gets invited to their houses to do homework together. Angela fears her peers will find out they are state wards. Because of the negative stereotypes and rejection that occur after discovery, she is careful to keep that fact hidden.

The three sisters settle into a routine at the Kowalskis' and get comfortable. While the couple does not mistreat Angela and her sisters, as in every former foster home except for the Wilson house, the Kowalskis do not treat the girls as family members. For example, Yvette and Henry often go out to eat with her siblings and their families on Sundays, and while Yvette's nieces, nephews, and Gary go, the Carcieri girls stay at home. This practice contributes to Angela's sense of inferiority.

That summer, after Teresa graduates from middle school, she moves to a different foster home with only a one day notice. Teresa looks distraught when she hugs Angela goodbye, which upsets Angela, too, so she questions Yvette.

"Why did Teresa move?"

"It just wasn't a good fit; Teresa was too old for us."

"But you knew her age before we came."

"I know, but it didn't work out."

Angela discovered the truth later. Fifteen-year-old Teresa's innocent need for affection from a mother figure frightened Yvette. The woman misinterpreted it, thinking Teresa was sexually attracted to her. Yvette's adverse reaction and rejection hurt Teresa, and Angela resented her foster mother because of it.

After Teresa's departure, Angela figures it will be only a matter of time before she and Margie go, too. She is cautious, trying to avoid mistakes and to make herself valuable to the family. When the Kowalskis are out, Angela does things intended to surprise and please them. For example, on a Saturday, she washes and waxes the floor of their huge eat-in kitchen on her hands and knees with a scrub brush. The scrubbing, rinsing, and waxing of this self-assigned chore take over three hours to complete. Her accomplishment pleases Angela, and she cannot wait for the Kowalskis to come home and find their surprise.

When they arrive home, Angela is smiling. She expects her surprise will thrill the Kowalskis'. When they say nothing, the girl speaks.

"Do you notice anything different?"

"What do you mean?" Yvette's eyes dart around the room, looking for a clue.

"What did you break?"

"No; nothing! Do you see something good?"

"Just tell us what it is."

"I washed and waxed the floor. Doesn't it look good?"

"Oh, you did? How come?"

"I wanted to surprise you with something nice."

"Oh. Well, you didn't have to do that."

Angela goes into the bathroom and closes the door to screen her feelings.

The rest of the summer turns out much better. Henry and Yvette take Gary and the girls to the beach, picnics and the drive-in movies. Their outings are fun, and except for getting her first menstrual period, Angela has a fun summer. The girl has heard of menstruation, so she is not frightened. Her foster mother explains to Angela what is happening with her body and says she is a young lady now. Angela does not want what comes with the title.

That summer is significant, too, because Angela meets Sharon, a girl her age who lives across the street. They become inseparable, best friends. Her new friend is an only child, and her parents spoil her. Angela benefits from this because when her parents take Sharon somewhere, they take Angela, too. Sharon's invitations for Sunday night suppers are a favorite treat for Angela. They feast on roasted-chicken sandwiches on fresh Kaiser rolls and even have potato chips and giant chocolate-chip cookies from the bakery. Angela thinks it must be nice to be an only child.

Similar to most homes, the Kowalskis have rules for the girls. Friends may not play inside, so unless they are playing outdoors, Angela plays at Sharon's house. The cupboards and refrigerator are off-limits, and the only food permitted is what

Yvette gives them. Still, they have enough to eat and do not go hungry here.

The rule Angela dislikes the most is that she may leave the table only when she has finished everything on her dish, even if she finds the food distasteful. This rule brings back memories of the dreaded oatmeal, but Henry and Yvette have no paddle. Angela often finds it challenging to eat things she dislikes and, sometimes, she will be at the table for two hours trying to force-feed herself. Sweet Margie comes to the rescue. The Kowalskis' habit is to retire to their bedroom after dinner to talk in private, so Angela and Margie are alone in the eat-in kitchen. One evening, after being at the table for a long time, forcing herself to swallow the food she hates, Angela gets up to go to the bathroom. The girl fills her mouth with as much food as it can hold so she can spit it into the toilet, but a mound of the dreaded turnips remain on her plate, stone cold by now. Angela does not dare throw the food into the trash because Yvette checks the wastebasket. When she returns to the table, her plate is empty, and Margie is smiling at her.

"Thank you so much!" The empty dish is a welcome sight.

"Why are you thanking me? I didn't eat it; your fairy godmother came when you were in the bathroom, and she ate it for you."

"Well, be sure to thank her for me." Both sisters laugh. From then on, whenever Angela must eat the food she hates, Margie suggests she go to the bathroom.

"Maybe your fairy godmother will come."

The girls eat the same inexpensive food as their foster parents, such as fried bologna, meatloaf or macaroni with jarred sauce. Yvette is a good cook, though, and the food is flavorful. The Polish meals are Angela's favorite. Yvette prepares kielbasa, sauerkraut with noodles, and pierogies. Polish bread from the bakery, delicious hard-crusted rye, accompanies most dinners. Henry cuts the loaf with a huge knife he calls "the weapon," making the girls laugh. While remembering the food, it strikes Angela how prominent an emotional role food has always had in her life.

* * *

During that same summer, Angela spends much of her time with Gary and comes to love her little foster brother. Too, she and Margie make other friends in the neighborhood, and they spend summer evenings playing Simon Says, Hide and Seek, and other such games in the street. Angela feels the most normal while playing with the neighborhood kids. The girl recognizes she isn't much different from the other kids, even if she is a state ward. Angela loves these memories.

The boy next door gets in the habit of playing badminton in the Kowalskis' driveway on weekday afternoons with Angela, who loves competition. She often wins the games, which thrills her. A few children tease the two players.

"Bobby and Angela, sitting in a tree, k-i-s-s-i-n-g," they chant.

"We're just friends!" Angela hopes the other kids assume the exercise of the game causes her flushed face.

"No, Bobby loves you!"

"I do not! She's too skinny." Angela had not realized she still looked skeletal.

In late August, just two months after Teresa's departure, Gary goes to live with his biological mother. His departure devastates Angela. She worries whether Gary's mother is taking proper care of him because she had been neglectful in the past, causing the Department of Children, Youth, and Families (DCYF) to remove Gary from her home. Angela misses him and remembers the little guy often.

Angela loses too many people who matter to her, except for Margie, who has been the only constant in Angela's life. Margie is a dear, innocent child, and her big sister is protective of her. After Gary leaves, Angela decides not to risk getting attached to anyone else she might lose.

When school resumes, Angela focuses on her sixth-grade schoolwork and continues to do well. Her shyness has diminished from what it was, so she makes friends with more of her schoolmates than last year. The self-conscious child enjoys wearing school uniforms because she does not have the fashionable clothes her classmates do. Angela joins the Girl Scouts after she turns eleven that December and her self-esteem improves.

The biweekly visits with Luigi and her siblings continue, and she becomes closer to her fifteen-year-old sister, Anna. Angela, who longs to be a teenager, thinks Anna is gorgeous and idolizes her. Anna is sweet to Angela and Margie, and they visit her at the foster home in which she has lived for several years. Their two youngest siblings, eight-year-old Katherine and six-year-old Donald, live in the same household with Anna.

Donald, the youngest, is a cute, mischievous little imp. Katherine, who is quiet and well-behaved, has an exotic beauty that Angela admires. Their foster parents are a couple in their fifties, who are good people, and Angela is fond of them. They take the girls, including Angela and Margie, to Portuguese feasts and other social events they attend.

On one of their regular visits with their father, Luigi informs his children he and Alice have found an apartment large enough for the family. He asks the children if he can borrow the money from their meager bank accounts to get the new place so they can be together again. Angela can see Luigi's awkwardness in having to ask, and she feels sorry for him.

From birth on, each time his children receive cash from any of their Carcieri relatives for a present, along with Grandma L.'s annual $2.00 birthday gift to each child, Luigi puts the money into the bank for them. Their understanding is the funds are for when they get older, and they should not spend them for any reason. None of the children know the balance in the account, but Angela assumes it cannot be much. They agree to loan their father the money. Several siblings, including Margie, think this means they will go home to live with Luigi. Angela knows better, and she tries to warn Margie not to get up her hopes. Too, she knows he will never repay them, but she is okay with it. Angela enjoys being able to help her father.

Within a few weeks, Luigi and Alice move into a large, three-bedroom, third-floor flat. They fill the ample space with lovely, used furniture their Carcieri relatives have donated. Angela sees it as a mansion compared to their two-room apartment. They take none of the children home to live with them, and Angela does not ask why. She expected as much. Once in a while, the children have sleep-overs at Luigi's, and they spend a week there in the summers. The new house even has a small backyard with grass and a tree, perfect for Angela to sit under and read her beloved books.

At the Kowalskis', beginning that winter and continuing the following years, Angela helps Henry with snow shoveling, yard work, stripping wallpaper, and cleaning apartments when tenants move. Sometimes, Angela and Henry saw huge logs on a two-person saw to feed the wood stove in the unfinished basement. Henry teases her and laughs.

"I'm helping you to build big, strong muscles."

"But I don't want big muscles; I'm a girl! It's bad enough I beat the boys in my class at arm wrestling,"

Angela has noticed the boys getting upset when this happens, and she has stopped challenging them. The message has come across: girls showing their physical strength is unacceptable. Boys consider them the weaker sex. Angela hates that term and wants to scream and prove them wrong. But being accepted by her peers is more important to her now.

Regardless, spending time with Henry is enjoyable. He is fun-loving, often jokes with her, and they get along well. When they watch the *Twilight Zone* on television in the darkened living room on Friday nights, Henry takes off his shoe and tosses it towards Angela at the most suspenseful part of the program. Angela jumps and screams, and he laughs with glee.

Yvette gets a part-time job waitressing, at night and on weekends, so she is home much less. She instructs the girls what to do if she is at work.

"If I'm not here when you get home from school, just wait in the yard."

"Even when it's raining or cold?"

"Then wait in the basement."

"What if we need the bathroom?"

"You can use the bucket in the basement. I'll leave a roll of toilet paper there, and you can empty the bucket and clean it when I get home."

As in every other foster home, the girls do not get a house key. Angela finds Yvette's solution insulting, and she resents having to use a bucket as if she were less than human. Earlier, resentment was a rare emotion for Angela, but she is experiencing it more often now. The girl cannot figure out why Yvette will not trust her to have a house key. It is nonsensical because the Kowalskis leave the girls alone in the house when they go somewhere. Angela may be a foster child, but she has never once stolen or even touched something off-limits.

Henry's mother, who lives on the floor above them, is a kind woman, and Angela develops a relationship with her. The girls call her "Baba," a short version of the Polish word for a grandmother. She teaches Angela how to play a song on her piano, an instrument Angela has always loved. After Baba teaches Angela how to play canasta (the woman's favorite card game), they spend time together playing cards and eating sweet, green, seedless grapes. The girl loves the one-on-one time she spends with Baba.

In her quest for attention, approval, and a sense of belonging, Angela visits Yvette's parents and her married sister. They live in the same town, and Angela enjoys walking, so she visits them often during the summers. Both Yvette's and Henry's parents treat Angela well, and she loves the ice cream sundaes Yvette's mother serves on her visits, but Baba is Angela's favorite foster relative.

During their first year at the Kowalski house, Robbie, the girls' brother, who is a career Marine, takes them to his home for the day. He lives in military housing on the nearby base with his wife and a young son. Angela loves those days. They are attentive to her and her siblings. One day, she is ill, so they put Angela on their bed to rest, giving her their son's soft and cuddly stuffed dog to hold. When they see how much the toy comforts Angela, they buy her one and give it to her the next time she comes to visit. Their kindness touches Angela, and their gift brings her much joy.

The children spend the day with Robbie and his family around three or four times, then the visits stop. Angela does not know why but is guessing her brother might have transferred to a different base. It bothers the little girl that Robbie said nothing to her and, again, neglected to say goodbye. She reconciles this oversight by assuming it was not possible.

Then, the week before Christmas, one year after arriving at the Kowalskis', Angela's older sisters, Evie, Laurie and Mary come for a surprise visit. Angela shrieks with delight when she sees her beloved Mary, whom she had not seen in the six years since their mother died, and embraces her with a bear hug. The visit is short, but Evie continues to visit the girls.

Angela wonders why none of her Carcieri relatives ever visit her or her siblings. Auntie Concetta accompanied Luigi to the Children's Center once or twice. But, none of them have ever visited the children at their foster homes, taken them out anywhere, or brought them to their homes. As a child, Angela concludes they dislike her and her siblings and wonders if it is because they are state wards. The girl's resentment over their neglect is growing.

Although she does not see her relatives often, Angela has plenty to keep her occupied. Yvette has several nieces and nephews whom Angela babysits when their parents go out for the evening. One evening, when eleven-year-old Angela is babysitting an infant and a two-year-old, the baby awakens and screams. Angela holds her and does everything she can to soothe the child, from changing her diaper to giving her a bottle, walking and rocking her, and patting her back, but the child will not stop wailing. Angela is overwhelmed and does not know what to do. She even tries singing to the baby. Not knowing what else to do, the girl lays the infant back in her crib, but she continues her loud crying. Angela is weeping, too, and worrying the baby might be sick.

None of the adults have told her where they will be. In desperation, Angela calls the telephone operator to get the phone number of a nightclub the Kowalskis frequent. Although the operator helps, Angela cannot find either the Kowalskis or the children's parents. At last, the baby falls asleep, but Angela is stressed and too young to have such responsibility. From then on, the girl insists on having a phone number where she can reach the parents when she is babysitting.

Sometimes, the parents of the children she watches give Angela a few dollars, or she does chores for them to earn money. Too, she and Margie get a few dollars in a birthday or Christmas card from the Kowalskis' relatives. Yvette holds this cash for them, each in a separate metal band-aid box in her bureau drawer. One day, Angela wants money for something at school, but Yvette says she does not have enough funds left.

"Why not?" Angela does not recall spending any money.

"Well, we went to the movies, had an ice cream cone last week, and we got Chinese food the other night."

Without ever informing Angela and Margie, Yvette was making withdrawals from the band-aid boxes for every treat the girls had. The sisters thought the Kowalskis were paying for them when they took them somewhere or bought them

SANDRA DUCLOS, Ph.D.

ice cream and takeout food. Angela could not believe Yvette
did this without asking the girls. She unclenched her teeth,
and for the first time, Angela speaks up on her and Margie's
behalf, telling Yvette she should have asked permission. The
next time Yvette says they are going somewhere, Angela questions Yvette.

"How much will it cost?"

"Around three or four dollars."

"I prefer not to go; I don't want to spend the money."

"Well, it's not your choice; you're coming with us."

While Angela's efforts to assert herself did not pay off or
cause Yvette to change how she handled their money, it still
made Angela proud. Finding her voice empowered her and
was significant progress for the passive girl.

10

THE KOWALSKIS: PART 2

In the late spring of sixth grade, Angela makes her Confirmation, professing her faith, and taking the Confirmation name, Immaculata. The young girl chose this unusual name to erase the stain she thinks is on her soul from the rape. Yvette is working that Sunday, and, once again, Luigi and Alice say they cannot attend the ceremony. Angela was expecting as much, but still had hope when she invited her father. Angela's resentment toward Luigi is growing.

Henry, Baba, and Margie go to the church ceremony, and it relieves Angela to have them there for her. She has developed genuine and meaningful relationships with Baba and Henry, and they enrich her life. Those relationships contribute to her increased self-esteem. Henry even takes a few pictures of the Confirmation. Angela wears another borrowed white dress and veil, but this time, the dress nearly fits. With being confirmed, she believes she has a fresh start in life because the nuns told her she is now a soldier of Christ.

That summer, Yvette convinces the state to send the girls to summer camp for a week. Angela does not want to go. She is still shy and uncomfortable around strangers. Also, the child is still wetting the bed, and Angela fears the other campers will find out and make fun of her. When she asks Yvette to bring extra sheets, she refuses.

"You'll just have to wash your sheets and hang them out when you wet them."

"But the other kids will laugh at me."

"Well, then maybe you should stop wetting the bed."

Her embarrassment causes Angela to lie to her cabin's counselors, telling them she has a kidney problem. She uses the same excuse when her peers ask her why she washes her sheets. No one mentions it afterward.

Connie is a gawky and skeletal, six-foot-tall girl in her cabin who has no social skills, and everyone makes fun of her. Angela sympathizes with Connie, partners with her in games and on lines when nobody else will, and defends her against others' verbal attacks.

At a camp softball game, Angela is standing near the home plate because she is next up to bat. The current batter hits the ball and flings her bat, knocking Angela unconscious. When she awakens in the infirmary, Connie is sitting by her bed, concerned for Angela. The nurse said Connie refused to leave her bedside. Angela recovers with no adverse consequences. She still hates camp.

That same summer, during one of her Saturday visits with Luigi, he is driving along with six of his children piled into the back seat of his car. Teresa is sitting in the front between her father and step-mother. Luigi's oldest child resembles her mother to a remarkable degree, and he has always favored Teresa. She and Angela are arguing during the drive, one as loud as the other. Angela has grown much more feisty and is holding her own with Teresa.

"Angela, why did you leave your glass in the sink after I cleaned everything?"

"I didn't leave it there."

"Yes, you did. I saw you drinking, and I had to clean it. You need to pick up after yourself."

"Well someone else must have left a glass because I washed mine. Besides, you're not the boss of me. Stop telling me what to do. You think you can boss everyone. I'm sick of it!"

"I'm older, so you have to listen to me."

"No, I don't! You think you're so smart! You're not my mother!"

"Shut up!" Luigi yells. His aggressive tone startles Angela. While he shouts, without warning, he turns and backhands Angela across the face very hard. Angela's face stings, but she refuses to cry. After the first few seconds of shock wear off, she flushes with humiliation and, within an instant, a surge of anger arises in her. At that moment, Angela hates Luigi with a frightening intensity. She has an urge to shout, "I hate you!" But she restrains herself. The ride continues in silence, and Angela neither speaks to nor looks at Luigi for the rest of the day. The sulking girl stays to herself and does not talk to anyone. No one even notices. Angela does not hold a grudge, but her feelings for her father have changed in a slight, inexplicable way. The assault was an isolated incident, and the only time Angela remembers Luigi striking any of his children.

In seventh grade, it surprises Angela to be one of the most popular kids in her classroom. Since emerging from her shell, the girl is outgoing and is friends with everyone in her class, getting lots of invitations for sleep-overs and such. The girl's confidence has skyrocketed compared to what it was in earlier years. She and her friends walk everywhere and, at twelve years old, she develops her first crush on a tall boy in her class. This year, she has an active social life, but things are rocky at home.

Since Yvette is working most evenings, Henry relies more on Angela to do little things for him, such as making him a cup of coffee. Angela sits and chats with him in his basement workshop where he does woodworking jobs to supplement his income. Henry teaches her about his work and discusses his philosophy on life. Angela gets the impression that Yvette dislikes the time Henry and Angela spend together and the father-daughter fondness they have developed. The woman's behavior toward Angela changes, and she criticizes the girl, making fun of how she dresses and what she says. Yvette's bullying confuses Angela. Although she says nothing, it relieves Angela when Yvette goes to work.

One day in early June, Yvette's sister-in-law is visiting Yvette, and they are chatting.

"I need to find a dress for a wedding."

"Who's wedding is it?"

"Michael, my coworker. He's a nice guy, and we've worked together for years. The fiance, Jane, is gorgeous. Mike told me she has a great family; they used to foster two little sisters, just like you do."

"Oh, yeah?"

"What is Jane's last name?" Angela interrupts their conversation.

"Her name is Jane Wilson. Why? Do you know her?"

"Yes! Oh my gosh! Margie and I lived with her family!" Angela is trying hard to contain her excitement but is losing the battle.

Two days later, Angela receives a telephone call from Jane, whom she has not talked to in five years. Jane says it thrills her to have found the girls, and she wants Angela and Margie to attend her wedding in a few weeks. Angela cannot wait to see the Wilsons again and counts the days. At the reception, the family greets the Carcieri sisters, but Angela does not get the same warmth from them as she expected, except for Jane. The wedding is not the joyful reunion with the Wilsons the little girl imagined in her daydreams. Further, Angela is unaware that this event is the last time she will see Lena and Joe.

One month after her wedding, Jane takes Margie and Angela out for pizza and brings them to her apartment on another occasion, but the visits stop. Angela does not know why, and Yvette will not allow her to call Jane.

"Jane will call you if she wants to see you. Don't be bothering her."

On a Sunday in July, the Kowalskis take Angela and Margie for a day at the beach, along with Baba, and Henry's sister and her family. When they arrive, they have a car full of beach equipment and food to unpack, and everyone is in and out of the car, retrieving everything. When Angela clears the back seat of its contents, she slams the car door shut. To her horror, Henry's thumb is in the car door jamb. Angela apologizes to Henry, but Yvette screams at her.

"What's wrong with you? Don't you know enough to look before closing the door?

"I'm so sorry! I didn't see his thumb. It wasn't on purpose."

"Just get out of my sight!" Yvette spits out the hurtful words, and Angela sees hatred in her foster mother's eyes. The girl turns around to hide the tears welling up and heads toward the beach. Baba walks with her and puts her arm around Angela's shoulder.

"I know you didn't want to hurt Henry, and I can tell you feel terrible."

"It was an accident. But now Yvette hates me."

"Everyone has accidents sometimes. Yvette was just upset and didn't mean it. Don't worry; Henry will be fine." Baba joins Angela's band of angels that day.

*　　*　　*

It relieves Angela when Yvette decreases her criticisms. The girl continues to do well at school and, to her surprise, she wins a school-wide essay contest on Pope John XXIII's life. Angela is proud of her accomplishment. Her faith has deepened, and she still goes to God with everything in her life. Angela feels so blessed, and she thanks God for everything she has.

But, the now thirteen-year-old is having questions about the Catholic religion, which the nuns at school cannot answer to her satisfaction. For example, why can't women be priests, and why do nuns have to take a vow of poverty but priests do not? Angela struggles with a belief in hell. It baffles her how anyone can consider it justice to condemn an imperfect being to torture for eternity. Spending hours lying in bed at night and trying to grasp eternity gives her insomnia and a colossal headache.

Regardless of Angela's questions on Catholicism, her faith in God does not waver, and she can distinguish between the two. Angela decides she wants to devote her life to God. When she learns that the religious order of her school nuns has a novitiate with a high school juniorate, she investigates. The juniorate, starting in the ninth grade, prepares girls for the novitiate to become nuns (even though she prefers to be a priest). Angela applies to the program and gets accepted.

The last week in August before ninth grade, Angela arrives at her new home. The convent is two hours away and one state north of her town. She cannot wait to get there and start her new life. Angela wants to emulate the saints whose stories the girl has admired. She also is concerned whether she will be good enough to be a nun and does not know what to expect there. The school is a regular, girls-only Catholic school with kids mostly outside the juniorate attending. Life in the convent is rigorous and disciplined, reminding Angela of the Children's Center.

There is no talking except during free time, a difficult rule for teenagers to keep. Mother Superior screens incoming and outgoing mail. Both the nuns and the other girls are too intense and gloomy for Angela's taste, and not much fun is happening here. Angela expects people to be joyful serving God and following their vocations, and wonders why the Sisters are not happy. But her spirits lift when she receives two letters from Henry, and his thoughtfulness touches her.

One day, Mother Superior reads one of Angela's letters from Sharon, who talks of going to a dance with a boy, and the nun accuses Angela of being boy crazy. Sister arriving at such a false conclusion shocks Angela. After that, Mother Superior pays special attention to Angela, watching her at prayer and questioning the other nuns as to their impressions of her. The girl believes the nuns are holier than she and, hence, superior to her. So, although Angela always looks people in the eye while conversing with them, when she passes the nuns, she smiles and then gazes downward to show humility and deference to them.

When one nun tells Mother Superior that Angela will not look the sisters in the eye when she passes them, Mother Superior accuses Angela of dishonesty.

"If you have a clear conscience, you aren't afraid to look people in the eye."

"I'm not afraid, Sister. I'm looking you in the eye right now."

"Well, we see something different, and I made my decision."

Angela's heart sinks, and she vows to herself to improve. But, she never gets the chance. In mid-December, three and one-half months after she arrived, Mother Superior informs Angela she will leave this afternoon to return home.

"This is not the right place for you."

"May I say goodbye to my friends?"

"No, that's not a good idea. One of the senior girls will help you pack. Try to be a good girl now. God bless you."

Angela wants to hide because of the rejection, being inadequate, and failing to finish what she started. But, at the same time, she breathes a sigh of relief. In her heart, she knows Mother Superior made the right decision.

Margie is glad to have her sister back, and so is Henry. Yvette informs Angela her school agreed to take her back after Christmas vacation, so long as she does not discuss the juniorate with her peers. When Angela returns to school, most of her classmates welcome her back. The girls want to know her experiences while she was away, but Angela tells them she agreed not to discuss it. While Angela immerses herself in her school work, life continues as if the girl never left.

Toward the end of January, Anna gives birth to her first child. Sophia is the cutest little, chubby-cheeked, bald baby Angela has ever seen. The baby's father thinks Anna looks like the famous movie actress, Sophia Loren, so they name their baby after the actress. This adorable infant is the first child of the Carcieri siblings and Luigi's first grandchild. Everyone in the family is over the moon for her. Angela loves being an auntie and intends to give Sophia the most love she can. The new auntie is eager to spoil this little cutie.

Soon after the excitement surrounding Sophia's birth, the teachers hold another school-wide essay contest to welcome the new school principal. This Mother Superior will come from France, and they want to make a good impression. The winner of the competition will read his or her composition to the entire school at the huge welcoming ceremony they are planning. To the dismay of several classmates, Angela's essay wins. While she is excited her piece won, she dreads having to read it to the entire school and the church dignitaries at the ceremony.

Angela's social life continues as it was before she left for the novitiate. A local drugstore and soda fountain with booths in the back is the hangout for her and her friends. One guy in the group, George, attracts Angela's attention. Three years older, he is a senior in a boys' Catholic high school. He is everything she is not: confident, witty, outgoing, and comfortable with himself. George and Angela first met when she was only ten years old, and he was a paperboy on her street. A few years later, they had a group of friends in common, and he used to flirt with her friend. Angela thought he was cocky and conceited, and she disliked him. The girl has had a drastic change of heart since then. She realizes he likes her, too. One day, their group of friends is at the drugstore talking. George has to leave and says goodbye, heading to the front of the store. In a few minutes, he returns with a fountain glass of cola. "Here." He places the glass of cola in front of Angela. "This will keep you company until I get back." She cannot stop smiling.

When Angela's classmates continue to question her on the juniorate, she succumbs to their badgering and answers them with honesty. The girl contracts a virus during the winter and is out of school for a few days. When Angela returns to school, she senses a palpable tension in the air. No one greets her or speaks to her. As they line up in the schoolyard to enter school, none of her classmates even look at her. With her stomach in knots, she wonders what is happening. Whatever is amiss, she knows it cannot be positive.

After morning prayer, the teacher gives the students an assignment and asks Angela to come with her. They go to the principal's office. While Angela was out sick, her teacher had grilled her classmates, trying to discover whether Angela had discussed the juniorate. Sister has a whole list of negative things the girls told her Angela reported; many statements are correct, and a few are not. Item by item, Sister asks if Angela said each one, and then she translates for the French-speaking Mother Superior, who scrutinizes Angela and her reactions the entire time. Then the Sisters announce they will discuss whether they will allow the girl to continue going to school there, and will let her know their decision by the end of the day.

Nausea overtakes Angela as she worries over the outcome. But her most profound pain comes from the betrayal and lies by people she thought were her friends. Angela admonishes herself.

How could I be so stupid?

At lunchtime, Sister tells Angela to come to the convent with her. Her teacher states they will give her a choice. She may finish the ninth grade here and graduate in June, but only if she stands in front of her class and admits her juniorate stories were lies.

"But I didn't lie!"

"Yes, you did, and you will admit it to the class and apologize, or you can choose expulsion. Also, you are not to discuss this with any of your peers. If you say one word about any of this to them or question them in any way, we will expel you on the spot."

The last thing Angela wants is to go to another new school with only a few more months until graduation. That evening, Angela tells Yvette what happened.

"It doesn't matter whether you lied."

"But it's not fair!"

"You do what they are telling you to do."

"Then I'll be lying when I tell the class everything I said was a lie."

"You disobeyed by discussing it, and now you have to face the punishment." Yvette's coldness floors Angela.

The next day, the kids still shun Angela. Mrs. Kowalski had called the school in advance to assure the nuns Angela will apologize, so her teacher is ready. After morning prayer, Sister announces Angela has something she wants to say to her classmates.

The self-conscious and insecure fourteen-year-old, who struggles with always needing to be perfect and fears looking flawed, stands in front of her classmates, shaking and hesitant. Every droplet of moisture evaporates from her mouth, leaving her so parched that she doubts she can even speak. Angela's heart is pounding so hard that she worries whether others can hear it. Too, the girl is hoping her voice doesn't shake as much as the rest of her body. Mustering every ounce of courage she has, Angela tells the class everything she said about the juniorate was a lie, and she is sorry.

Angela wishes she could evaporate, as her self-esteem has, and cease to exist. The girl wonders if the nuns know how torturous this ordeal is for her, or if they even care. One arrogant, insensitive female classmate stands up and speaks as if she is representing the entire class.

"We're willing to forgive Angela if she's really sorry and won't lie anymore."

Angela's angst from this entire, nightmarish experience gets transferred to that one girl, and it takes everything Angela has not to choke her. She cannot remember ever hating anyone so much as she does that callous girl at this moment.

* * *

Social life at school is nonexistent for Angela now. It reminds her of when she was at the Children's Center and was a loner. The girl gets through the rest of the school year by focusing on her work, and she seldom speaks to any of her classmates. Angela is carrying a boulder-sized grudge but does not realize she is hurting herself. Social interaction is now only with friends in her neighborhood or sneaking out to see George, whom the Kowalskis have forbidden her to see.

"He's too old for you," Yvette says.

"There's only one thing a seventeen-year-old boy wants from a fourteen-year-old girl," Henry preaches.

"Can't you just meet him, and you'll see he's not like that?"

"You might be right," Henry says, "but we said no, and now we have to stick by what we said."

Angela can't understand why they hold their position even after admitting they might be wrong. Henry's sister lives next door to the Kowalskis, and they have her husband spying on Angela whenever they leave the house and Angela is home. One night, when George picks her up on a side street, Henry's brother-in-law follows them in his station wagon. George zig-zags from one road to another, and the man gives up, recognizing he has blown his cover. From then on, when she sneaks out to see George, Angela goes around the side of the house opposite from where Henry's sister lives.

To this day, Angela laughs when she recalls the evening she and George were sitting in his car, parked in front of the Kowalskis' house when they were out for the evening. Her foster parents arrive home much earlier than expected. When Angela sees them pull into the driveway, she bolts out of George's car and runs up the front steps. While the Kowalskis are parking the car in the garage at the back of the house, Angela bangs on the front door (which they never use) for Margie to let her into the house. Then, she runs into her bedroom and does a speed change into her pajamas. When Angela realizes Yvette and Henry did not spot her in George's car, and she is not in any trouble, it exhilarates her.

In June, Angela graduates from ninth grade. As usual, her father and Alice do not attend the ceremony, and it still hurts, but Margie, Henry, and Baba witness her receiving her diploma. Angela appreciates their presence, but it bothers her to think she is not important enough for her father to attend. To celebrate, after the graduation ceremony, Henry and Baba take the girls out for a pizza at the restaurant where Yvette is working, and the Kowalskis and Baba each give Angela a gift. Angela recognizes them as blessings in her life.

It relieves the new graduate to be free of that school, those nuns and her former classmates. Angela looks forward to a fresh start at a new school next fall. She will attend the girls' Catholic high school in town and will be with only one of her former classmates, who is kind.

The summer flies by, and Angela begins tenth grade at her new school. On their first day, the students can wear street clothes instead of their usual uniforms. Angela is careful to look her best, spending hours getting ready and trying to apply eye makeup just as Yvette does. As Angela prepares to leave, Yvette looks at her and chuckles.

"You look like a frump."

"What's a frump?"

"Nothing, never mind."

Often, Yvette says something then refuses to explain what she means, which frustrates Angela. But from her tone and facial expression, the girl realizes Yvette insulted her. *Why didn't she try to help me instead of ridiculing me?* The deflated Angela heads to her first day of high school, wondering if she looks terrible.

Once at school, though, many new peers become her friends. Their genuine friendliness surprises Angela, and it helps soothe her anxiety and lessen her self-doubt. Another pleasant surprise is her homeroom teacher, a young, cheerful nun who makes learning fun. Best, though, are her secret meetings with George after school each day. He picks her up in his car, and they meet their friends at the drugstore.

"Where should we go today?"

"I don't have much time before Yvette becomes suspicious."

"Yes, but I want alone time with you."

He drives her to the park and takes her to the playground. He gets on a swing and pulls Angela onto his lap. They swing, use the slide, and run around like little kids, laughing and having a great time. Then they take a short walk. George pulls Angela close and wraps his arms around her.

"I need to tell you something." He is fidgeting and hesitating. "How do you feel about me?"

"You don't know? You mean everything to me!"

"I love you, Angela." He takes his school ring off and puts it on her finger. "Will you wear this to show everyone that you're mine?"

"Yes!" She feels the warmth of his love and the protection of his embrace. Angela wants to shout it to the world. She expects this will be a great year.

But during the fall, amid the Cold War, America's conflict with Russia is escalating. People are discussing Russian missiles that are ninety miles off our coast in Cuba, poised to launch in our direction. Henry builds a bomb shelter in his basement, and teachers tell their students to scrunch beneath their classroom desks if an air raid alarm sounds. Fear is rampant in the nation, and Angela has a few nightmares of bombs destroying the country.

In mid-December, George informs Angela he has joined the Marine Corps and will leave for boot camp the day after Christmas. This news shocks Angela because they have never discussed it. The military enlistment was George's impulsive attempt to show his father he could no longer control him. Angela cannot bear the thought of losing George. Seeing him over Christmas break is more difficult because she has to find a plausible reason to get out of the house. A last-minute Christmas shopping excuse buys her two hours with him a few days before Christmas.

"Will you wait for me?"

"Do you even have to ask? Of course, I will. You know I love you."

"And I love you. I can't stand the thought of being without you."

"I'll write every day, I promise."

When they embrace, Angela does not want to let go. He has been her safe place, and she revels in George's love for her. They both cry when they say goodbye, and Angela's world is crashing. She prays to God to keep him safe.

George writes to Angela, sending his letters to Sharon's house. Yvette, who snoops through Angela's things, even reading her diary, finds one of his letters. She reads it aloud at the dinner table in a dramatic voice, mocking what George has written while the rest of the family laughs. Angela's face flushes and the lump in her throat makes it difficult to swallow. She has to force herself to squelch the fury her foster mother has awakened in her and stop herself from lashing out at the cruelty.

Then, Yvette demands that Angela tell George to send his letters to the Kowalski street address. When his letters arrive, Yvette reads every one before giving them to Angela and screens the girl's outgoing mail to George.

Yvette Kowalski baffles Angela. Sometimes, her foster mother is compassionate and kind to her. For example, when the child was sad and self-conscious because she thought she was ugly, Yvette was the first person ever to tell Angela she was pretty. At other times, she is downright cruel. While the woman never beats her, Yvette's tongue cuts Angela with the sharpness and precision of a surgeon's scalpel, causing deep, bleeding wounds that go unstitched, fester and leave ugly scars on the teenager's psyche.

Sometimes, Yvette treats Angela as competition, and she bullies the girl. One night, as the family is eating dinner, Henry compliments Angela on something she has done well. Angela is in her old, hanging around-the-house clothes, and Yvette notices a tiny tear in the shoulder seam of the girl's blouse where it meets her arm. The woman makes fun of Angela and the way she dresses, laughs at her, and tears the sleeve right off Angela's arm, mortifying her. Henry has to intervene.

"That's enough."

"Why do you always have to take her side?"

Yvette goes into her bedroom and slams the door. Her comment surprises Angela, but it frightens her more.

If she thinks Henry is always taking my side over her, she'll hate me.

As a result, Angela's position is more vulnerable because Yvette controls everything. Despite Yvette's unpredictable behavior, Angela loves the Kowalskis. They are parents to her and often show they care. She believes this will be home until she marries.

Soon after Angela finishes tenth grade, and after five and a half years of living with the Kowalskis, Yvette tells the girls they will be leaving. The Kowalskis are adopting an infant,

129

and Yvette wants a fresh start by having just her, Henry, and the new baby as a family, she says.

Not only is Angela losing the Kowalskis and moving away from her best friend, Sharon, but she learns Margie will go home to live with Luigi and Alice, while she will move into the foster home where her sister Teresa is living. This move will be the first time she and Margie separate. Angela never saw this coming. Although the girl feels as if a truck ran her over, she puts on a smile.

"It's okay, I understand. I'm so happy that you're getting the baby you wanted for so long."

"Thank you. We still care for you and want you to be happy, too. We'll stay in touch, and you can visit us. I want you to meet the baby when we get her."

The teenager nods her head, but does not dare speak for fear of revealing her raw emotions, and exposing the hollow shell of a person who remains after they have ripped out her heart.

On her last night at the Kowalskis', Angela is lying awake in her bed with her sweet Margie asleep next to her for the last time. The girl prays to God to give her strength, knowing He is the only one who will never abandon her, and the only one she can trust. Angela is more sure of this than anything else in her life. Despite the horrible things she has endured, she has never blamed Him. Angela knows people cause evil things to happen, not God. Still, she cannot be angry at Yvette or Henry for their selfishness in this matter; her grief is too consuming.

So much loss at once overwhelms Angela, and she cannot sleep. As her silent tears flow, the heart-broken fifteen-year-old wonders who will watch over her little sister when she isn't there, and why Yvette and Henry are choosing a child whom they have never even met over her and Margie. The girl's thoughts will not stop.

Maybe love is just a fantasy and doesn't even exist, or I was right before, and I am just unloveable.

The next morning, when the Carcieri girls are departing, Yvette calls Angela aside and places a folded piece of paper in the girl's hand.

"This is something I wrote for you last year, and I want you to keep it and read it when you are lonely or afraid."

"Is it a letter?"

"No, it's a poem I wrote for you. Don't read it until later."

"Okay. Thank you."

They hug, and Angela gets into her social worker's car, headed to her new home.

Dedicated to Angela Carcieri:

Fearful Foundling

Dear frightened little girl nestled under our wing,
We wish we could predict what your future will bring.
We can only prepare you the best we know how,
And give you all the love that our hearts will allow.
No one could ever explain why it happened this way,
That your mother was taken, and you came here to stay.
We know in our hearts that we're really the same,
The only thing different is the family name.
So, try to remember as you go through the years,
Happiness can be yours if you shed all your fears.

By Yvette Kowalski
1962

11

MRS. JONES

Mrs. Jones's house is Angela's sixth placement in the ten years since she became a state ward. A divorced woman in her early fifties, Mrs. Jones lives with her elderly mother in the house where she was born and raised. She has three married children, several grandchildren, and two children still living at home: sixteen-year-old Maria and fourteen-year-old Steve. Mrs. Jones, who has been fostering children for decades, prefers teenagers to younger children. Besides Teresa and Angela, she has four other teenage state wards in her care (two sisters, another girl, and a boy), making a household of ten people.

The house is a two-story, single-family residence. They converted the basement into a kitchen and family room, and the attic has two bedrooms, providing four floors of living space. Angela is glad to reunite with Teresa and share one of the attic bedrooms with her.

To her astonishment, Angela's new home is on the side street that runs perpendicular to the Lundgrens' old house. Maria Jones is none other than the fantasy princess Angela used to watch! Upon seeing the Lundgren house at the head of the street, Angela has a flashback of Ted and panics. The terrified girl doubts she can live here. At first, Angela fears going outside, thinking another flashback will occur.

It floods Angela with relief when Teresa tells her the Lundgrens no longer live there. For a while, she avoids heading or even looking toward that house but finds it unavoidable. In time, repeated exposure helps Angela by decreasing her fear, and she stops having flashbacks. The nightmares continue for a while, though. When Angela's own screams awaken her in the middle of the night, the younger of the other two sisters in the adjoining attic bedroom yells in a nasty tone. "Shut-up, damn it!"

Angela is not the only one with a trying history. Mrs. Jones has endured much. As a young child, a vaccination left the woman with legal blindness. She has one glass eye, and her other eye is so damaged that Angela finds it challenging to look at her. As a teenager, Mrs. Jones attended the Perkins School for the Blind in Boston, where the famous Helen Keller got her education. The school equipped Mrs. Jones to be self-sufficient despite her disability. With her keen sense of hearing, she does not miss much. This ability was crucial when the woman had to raise her children as a single mother after divorcing her husband for being unfaithful multiple times.

Being a compassionate woman, Mrs. Jones is always more than willing to listen to the teenagers living with her. From boyfriend problems to personal emotions they struggle with, the woman tries to help by advising them. So, her state wards trust and confide in her. Angela, too, shares her feelings and concerns with Mrs. Jones until the day her foster mother divulges one of Teresa's confidences to her. From then on, Angela stops confiding in her. Despite that lapse, Mrs. Jones is a well-intentioned, dear woman, and Angela is fond of her.

Grandma Ricci is Mrs. Jones's mother. She was born in Italy and emigrated to the United States around fifty years ago, but still speaks with a heavy accent in broken English peppered with Italian words. At first, Angela cannot comprehend what the woman is saying. Quick to pick up many Italian words from the grandmother's conversations and those of her Carcieri grandparents, Angela comes to understand her. Grandma Ricci favors Teresa and Angela because they are Italian. For her advanced age, the woman is spry and cooks for the household. Every Thanksgiving, Grandma Ricci hosts her grandchildren and their families for dinner. With love, the woman spends days making hundreds of the most delicious chicken ravioli Angela has ever tasted. She then spreads clean, white sheets over most of the beds in the house and lays her homemade ravioli atop them to dry. Angela gets a kick out of seeing the ravioli-covered beds, and for an unknown reason, the sight of them makes her happy.

A laid-back environment permeates the Jones household. The children can come and go as they please, provided they tell Mrs. Jones where they will be. Their only chores are cleaning their bedrooms, doing their laundry, and taking turns setting the table and doing the dishes. Angela never had such freedom in other homes, and this placement is in radical contrast to the hyper-controlled environment at the Kowalskis'. Unlike several of Mrs. Jones's former teenagers, Angela handles her freedom well because she does not have a wild bone in her body. She is too afraid to do something she or others might consider wrong.

One thing remains the same as in her other foster homes, except for the Wilson house. They do not treat the foster kids the same as family members. Mrs. Jones's children, Maria and Steve, have no chores, and they sometimes have different food. Since money is tight, meals are inexpensive, such as hot dogs and beans, soup or Grandma Ricci's once-a-week, delicious macaroni and meatballs. A few times per week, only Maria (who has no food allergies or medical condition) gets a roasted chicken breast, instead of what everyone else is eating because she likes them.

Angela's earlier fantasy of Maria being doted on and getting what she wants is a reality. Maria and Steve, along with

Mrs. Jones, spend their time on the first floor of the house to watch television and entertain friends, while they relegate the foster children to the basement. Steve, who is warmer and more friendly than Maria, often hangs out in the converted cellar with the other kids, but Maria never does. On Thanksgiving, the foster children eat in the lower level kitchen with the toddlers while the rest of the family eats in the large, first-floor dining room.

That fall, Angela begins her junior year at her former high school. She has an active social life and lots of friends. Angela joins the school glee and drama clubs and enjoys her roles in plays. While public speaking gives her heart palpitations, she loves acting. Once Angela hits the stage, her pre-show jitters disappear as the actress loses herself in her role. She loves being someone else and feeds off the applause. Luigi never attends even one of her performances for either club.

On the week just before a big play, rehearsals run much later than usual, and Angela does not arrive home until 7:00 p.m. every day. She informed Mrs. Jones of this in advance. Dinner has long been over, but instead of saving Angela a plate of food, Mrs. Jones leaves a can of soup on the counter for her to eat. Nobody is there to sit with her when she eats, and no sandwich, bread or crackers are available—just a lone can of soup. When Angela arrives home on Friday night, she wants to cry when she sees that can of soup sitting on the counter for the fifth night in a row.

George and Angela continue writing back and forth with no one monitoring the letters. She is excited because they no longer have to date in secret when he comes home on leave from the Marines. Angela misses George so much, it aches. But, because of her young age, George understands she will date others. While Angela has an active social life and many dates, she allows no one to get close enough to get serious. Her heart belongs to George.

Grandma Ricci judges Angela's dates by their appetite for food, which Angela finds hilarious. If the guy loves to eat, she thinks he's delightful. If he is skinny and refuses food when she offers it, Grandma tells Angela to get rid of him.

"He no good. I no like him."

Angela loves that woman! She is tiny, but so feisty, strong of spirit, speaks without filters, and has a huge heart. She is the one who has kept Mrs. Jones' family afloat and is a force behind the scenes. Her daughter relies on her help and advice. Grandma is unaware that she is comical, and she often makes Angela laugh with her comments. The woman is forever trying to get Angela an Italian boyfriend, sometimes even her relatives. Angela knows she means well and just smiles and shakes her head.

*   *   *

In eleventh grade, Angela's homeroom teacher is a short, stocky, and jolly nun, who makes Angela laugh. She had Teresa as a student five years earlier and liked her, so Teresa's legacy benefits Angela. Several times during religion class, her teacher tells the girls never to use God's name in an exclamation, such as "Oh, my God," because that is taking the Lord's name in vain. In November, during English class, another nun entered the classroom to deliver a message to Sister. In response to what the messenger whispered in her ear, Sister exclaims,

"Oh, my God!"

We know it must be horrible news, and Sister shares the message with the class.

"I'm sorry to tell you, girls, but today, an unknown assailant has shot President John F. Kennedy in the head while he was riding in an open convertible on a parade route during his visit to Dallas, Texas. His condition is critical. Let's pray for him now."

The schools dismiss the children early that infamous Friday and President Kennedy dies later the same day. For the next three days, like most everyone she knows, Angela stays glued to the television in shock and disbelief. The girl has a terrible sense of loss. Her heart breaks, and she weeps when she sees little John-John salute his father's flag-draped casket as the funeral caisson passes, and she watches the riderless horse following it. Angela cries on and off for days, as does Mrs. Jones. According to the television news broadcasts, the entire nation is in mourning.

Despite the tragedy, as most young people do, Angela heals in a short time and moves forward. On her sixteenth birthday in December, Teresa surprises Angela with a birthday cake and present, and her sister's thoughtfulness touches her. Teresa has become a significant part of her life, and Angela not only appreciates her but sees her sister as a blessing. They both enjoy taking Sophia for the day whenever they can. Angela loves how Anna dresses the little girl in such adorable, frilly dresses and black patent leather shoes. Blonde ringlets now cover Sophia's once bald head. She is too cute for words and so sweet.

When Angela needs spending money so she can buy something for Sophia, get a soda with her friends, or go to dances, Teresa hires her sister to do her laundry. Angela scrubs Teresa's clothes on a washboard, rinses and hangs them on the clothesline in the spacious yard, then folds, irons, and puts them away for $2.75 per week. While it was not much money even then, it helps Angela get through the week. Teresa could have used Mrs. Jones washing machine, but, at her own expense, she is trying to help Angela. Her big sister is a lifesaver, and Angela knows she sacrifices for her, causing the girl to break her resolve not to trust or get attached to anyone ever again.

The younger of the other two sisters in the house is mean and hateful. She pretends to be Angela's friend, then talks behind her back. Although Angela is a virgin, the girl tells the boys in the neighborhood and in Angela's group of friends that Angela had sex with George. Those boys, who think the two girls are friends and confide in each other, believe the girl's lies. They then come on to Angela, thinking she is promiscuous. Steve is kind enough to tell Angela what has happened, so Angela makes it clear to everyone: the girl is neither her friend nor confidante, and she is a liar.

Another time, when Teresa and Angela go out for a rare restaurant meal, the girl tells Mrs. Jones they went out because Angela said Mrs. Jones was serving garbage for dinner. Mrs. Jones is angry and turns cold toward Angela. After she presses her foster mother to tell her what is wrong, Mrs. Jones repeats what the girl said. Again, Angela must try to repair the damage and defend herself against something she did not do.

Several similar events occur in which the girl tries to make Angela look bad, so she avoids that foster sister as much as possible. At least Angela can now stand up for herself. When she was younger, the girl did not defend herself. But Angela is getting stronger, more assertive, and more confident than ever. The fight is back in her.

Soon after Angela's sixteenth birthday, her social worker, whom she never sees, informs the girl, by phone, her official status has changed to being independent. Because she is sixteen years old, the state will no longer bear any responsibility for Angela. They will stop paying for her foster care, and they have released Angela from their custody. There is no forewarning, no preparation, no money to help get the child on her feet. The social worker does not ask what her plans are, and she gets no training for independent living. DCYF does not know whether Angela can find a job or even if she will be homeless. They wash their hands of her, based only on her age. Mrs. Jones then tells Angela she now must pay a weekly room and board fee if she wants to continue living there. Her foster mother is kind enough to give Angela a grace period for a month or until she gets a job, whichever comes first.

Angela is frantic in searching for work, but she keeps getting rejected because employers want someone full time. Angela, without a doubt, wants to finish high school, so she can only work late afternoons and evenings during the school year. Out of desperation, she takes a job in the local toy factory, which enables her to work part-time now, then full time in the summer.

While relieved she has a job, Angela hates the work. Her first assignment is on an assembly line. Her responsibility is to glue little squares and circles of hardened, molded watercolor paint onto a piece of cardboard as they move along a conveyor belt. It reminds Angela of the hilarious *I Love Lucy* television episode in which Lucy is working on an assembly line in a chocolate candy factory and cannot keep up, so she eats the candies and stuffs them into her clothes. The recollection of that episode causes Angela to laugh on the assembly line, and she gets several strange looks from her coworkers.

But this job is not funny. Angela fears she will go insane from the mind-numbing tasks. The girl tries to tolerate the work by singing and conversing with coworkers but is unsuccessful. Time continues to drag at a snail's pace. When Angela looks at the clock, checking for break time, only five minutes passed since the last time she looked. Angela has another year and a half to work before she graduates from high school. She knows she needs to find another job.

It relieves Angela when her assignment at the factory switches to painting eyeballs onto Mr. Potato Head's white plastic eyes. While the work is still mindless, she is not on an assembly line, and she must perform a few different operations to complete the job. Throughout the winter and spring, she does various other tasks, but she still hates the work. Angela dreads having to do this job full time in the summer. But she tolerates the work when she cannot find a different summer job. Angela misses spending carefree summer days at the beach with her friends, but she still has weekends to socialize.

During the spring, Angela gets a phone call from George. He announces he is shipping out to Okinawa the next morning, then going to Vietnam. Still early in America's active involvement in Southeast Asia, they have not even established a military base there yet. The evening news, though, reports on our country's escalating participation in the war. George is being sent over as part of a reconnaissance team.

"Please be careful. Promise you'll come back to me."

"You're the reason I will come back; I promise."

Angela's concern for George's safety consumes her, and she watches the news every night he is there. The newscasts report more and more war casualties and broadcast gruesome photos. Angela writes to George daily. Sometimes, with the long mail delays, she goes weeks without hearing from him and worries if he is alive. Angela pleads with God to keep him safe.

Sharon, her long-time best friend, maintains contact with Angela, but they seldom see each other because Angela now lives on the other side of town instead of across the street, and neither girl has a vehicle. Angela misses both Sharon and Jane Wilson, so she searches for and locates her former foster sister again. When they speak on the phone, Jane, who lives nearby, invites Angela to visit her. The woman is now a mother of three and leads a busy life. Angela visits Jane a few times, but they lose touch again. Angela guesses it must be because their lives are so different now.

* * *

One day that summer, Robbie surprises Teresa and Angela with a visit. Seeing her older brother thrills Angela; they last saw him six years ago. The girls do not mention their brother's absence from their lives and only discuss the present. It surprises Robbie to see Angela so grown. He was expecting her to be a child still. He remains in the Marine Corps but does not want to discuss that part of his life. Robbie is on military leave now and trying to enjoy his family, which has grown to three children instead of one. Angela tells him George is serving in Vietnam, and he shakes his head and changes the topic. This visit is the last time Angela sees Robbie for two more decades.

A nursing school accepts Mrs. Jones' daughter, Maria, into their program. She will begin studies for her R.N. degree at the local hospital in the fall. Mrs. Jones is so proud of her. Although Maria is a grade ahead of her, Maria's nursing plans make Angela realize she, too, needs to develop a career path. She does not want to remain a factory worker, and her drive to excel and need to prove herself are as strong as ever.

Since she now must buy her clothes, Angela becomes conscious of spending as little money as possible and is trying to save for upcoming senior year events. While her classmates are planning for college, Angela does not see it as a possibility for herself. None of her immediate family members have attended college, and her small, Catholic high school has no guidance or college counselors to advise her. Angela does not know that scholarships, student grants, and loans exist for which she might be eligible. She discusses the problem with Teresa.

"I want to go to college and will need a degree if I want a good job, but I can't afford it."

"I'd help you if I could, but I have no money. When you get a full-time job, maybe you can save and attend school at night."

"But even if I work full time, I can't afford the tuition on minimum wage, and I still need to support myself."

"Dad can't help, either. I'm sorry, I wish I could help. I wanted to go to college, too, so I know it stinks. Maybe you can go in a few years."

"Well, I guess I have no choice; I'll just wait."

In January of Angela's senior year of high school, Anna gives birth to her first son. When her sister asks her to be the boy's godmother, it thrills Angela. When she goes to the hospital to meet her soon-to-be godson, he steals her heart the moment she lays eyes on him. Anna has not decided on a name for the baby, so Angela suggests she call him David, and Anna agrees. Angela is so blessed to be his godmother. He ends up being a charming, little character who makes her laugh. Angela loves spending time with her little David, and he brings her great joy.

In February of her senior year of high school, one of Angela's teachers asks her why she has not requested a college letter of recommendation from her since the applications must be in by March 1st. Angela's face flushes.

"I'm not going to college."

"Why? What are you planning to do?"

"I am hoping to go to hairdressing school."

"Really? I can't picture that for you. Don't waste your potential Angela."

Angela knows she has disappointed Sister, but she does not know what else to do. Again, she feels deficient and wishes she could go to college, but she cannot, at least for now. She will not give up her dream of going someday, though.

Near the end of her senior year, Luigi, who had a high school graduation party for both Teresa and Anna, asks Angela if she prefers a bathing suit for her graduation gift or a party. His daughter wonders why he even asked her such a question, so tells him she will give him an answer later. Angela very much wants the party. She has never had one—not for a birthday or any other occasion. Angela remembers her sisters' graduation celebration and how the Carcieri relatives came, gave Teresa and Anna envelopes with money in them, and how much fun everyone had dancing and laughing. She sure could use those money gifts. She discusses it with Teresa.

"Why do you think Dad asked me if I prefer a graduation party or a bathing suit for my present? Why doesn't he throw the party without asking?"

"I guess he didn't know whether you want a party."

"Of course, I do! Who would prefer a bathing suit to a party?"

"You should ask him."

"My guess is he gave me a choice because he can't afford the party. Between the food and liquor, a party will be much more expensive than one bathing suit."

"But then he shouldn't have offered a party if he can't afford it. If you want the party, tell him." Angela is sure Luigi has no money, so she calls her father and says she prefers the bathing suit. Luigi sounds relieved.

For the first time, her father attends a significant event in Angela's life. Luigi and Alice come to her high school graduation, as do Teresa and the Kowalskis. Yvette and Henry give Angela her first suitcase as a present. They say she will need it to go with them to an island off the coast on one weekend this summer. Their long-time friends, whom Angela knows, bought a massive, historic hotel on the island and invited the Kowalskis for a weekend, agreeing to include Angela. This gift thrills Angela. No one has ever given her something so grand. Angela and the Kowalskis stay close, and she visits them often.

As usual, the summer after graduation passes in a flash. Angela is working full time at the toy factory and is on the lookout for better paying and less boring work. She investigates hairdressing schools, but tuition, even for one year, is unaffordable. Angela knows she must find a better job to increase her income and further her education. The girl is only making ends meet. Teresa suggests they might share a small apartment for less money than they are paying to Mrs. Jones, and they agree to try.

The sisters find a cute and clean three-room, furnished, second-floor flat, and the landlords are a lovely couple who live on the first floor. Teresa and Angela move out of Mrs. Jones's house, thanking her for her help, and stay in touch with her for the rest of her life. She was a dear woman, whom both girls loved. Teresa says the woman saved her life. When she first went to Mrs. Jones's house after leaving the Kowalskis, Teresa was depressed. Mrs. Jones took the time to show an interest in her and spent hours talking and listening to the girl, helping her out of her depression. Teresa named her only daughter after Mrs. Jones.

Angela and her best friend, Sharon, have not talked over the past several weeks. Sharon has one excuse or another when Angela calls. So, Angela drops by her house unannounced. Sharon does not let Angela through the door, saying she is ill. She is acting strange and even looks weird. That evening, Angela calls Sharon's mother to find out what is going on with her friend.

"Sharon had a breakdown last month, and we had to hospitalize her. The doctors diagnosed her with schizophrenia and medicated her with heavy doses of antipsychotic drugs. She's been home for only a few weeks, but she isn't doing well."

"Oh my gosh! I'm so sorry. What can I do?"

"I don't know. We don't think we can keep Sharon at home much longer."

"Why?"

"Sharon is paranoid and refuses to leave the house. Your visit upset her because she didn't want you to see her this way. So, I'm asking you not to visit her anymore."

"But what if I can help her by talking to her? I'm her best friend. I can try to get her out of the house to go for a ride or something."

"Please respect my wishes on this. I'm only trying to keep Sharon calm. I will call to keep you updated on her progress and let you know when she's ready to see you. Until then, it's best if you don't contact her. I'm sorry to do this. I know you love her, and this upsets you, but I must do what Sharon wants."

When they hang up, Angela drops to her knees and cannot focus or sleep for the next week. She can't stop crying or thinking about her friend. Sharon has repeated psychiatric admissions, and their relationship is never the same. Angela tries to reach out several times, but Sharon continues to reject her. The girl's heart breaks for her tormented friend, and she still misses the person Sharon used to be before mental illness robbed her of her life. Angela prays for Sharon daily.

Sharon's tragedy makes Angela even more aware of what a blessed life she leads. She determines to make the most of it and live with joy. Teresa helps make that possible. Although her sister is five years older than she, Teresa often takes Angela out with her, introduces her to her friends at the local restaurant where she works full time, gives her rides or lets her borrow her car, and provides Angela with the attention, affection, and sense of family she needs. They split their living expenses, share in the household chores, and grocery shop together. George and Teresa goof around when he comes home on military leave, and they become good friends.

Too, the sisters form a bond with their landlady and her family, and they often play cards together. The landlady is Italian. Once a week, when she makes spaghetti and meatballs, she sends a plate upstairs to the Carcieri girls. Angela laughs and wonders if the love of feeding people imprints on the Italian DNA.

Overall, Teresa and Angela delight in being on their own and no longer living as outsiders in someone else's house. For the first time in her life, Angela is independent and free, and she loves the freedom, the little apartment she and Teresa share, and their life together. The two sisters get along well and have so much fun. They often fill their tiny apartment with laughter. They are best friends and confidantes. Most important to them, they are living in a place where they belong. For the first time since their mother's death, Teresa and Angela finally are at home.

12

TYING UP LOOSE ENDS

After serving four years of active duty, including two tours of duty in Vietnam, George gets his honorable discharge from the U.S. Marine Corps. It relieves the couple that George returned home in one piece, and they do not want to wait to begin their lives together, so they set a wedding date.

Angela's conflicted relationship with Luigi, filled with resentment that has been building for years, comes to a head one month before her marriage. Luigi and Angela have a long-delayed and difficult conversation. She confronts her father on his neglect and selfishness over her lifetime.

"Why didn't you allow decent people to adopt us kids so we could have lived in good homes and had a shot at happy lives? Things could have been so different, especially for the little ones."

"I wanted you for myself. You were my kids."

"But you didn't have us!"

"You were still my kids, and I tried"

"Why were you never there for me?"

"What do you mean? I was always here if you needed me. All you had to do was ask."

"Really? How many times did I ask you to come to one of my plays or concerts when I was a kid? Didn't I ask you to come to my First Communion, Confirmation and ninth grade graduation, and to see me in my prom dress? Do I need to continue?"

"I did the best I could."

"Then why was my high school graduation the only significant event you ever attended in my entire life? Do you know what your absence did to me? Do you know how much it hurt every single time you weren't there?"

Luigi cannot answer. He tries to defend himself by reminding Angela what he did for his children: paying child support, buying them birthday and Christmas presents, visiting with them, taking them to the beach and such, and keeping them in his life. He never apologizes. They both say things in anger, and Angela, now crying, tells her father she does not want him at her wedding.

Angela is three weeks shy of twenty years old when Henry Kowalski walks her down the aisle in her stunning white gown and veil. At her insistence, they tailored her dress to fit her to a tee. Although she is still young, Angela has no doubts when marrying George. He was and shall ever be her "one and only" love. George and Angela's wedding reception is small but lovely. None of the Carcieri relatives show up, although she invited them. Angela assumes they are showing their solidarity with and support for Luigi. Only one first cousin, Auntie Concetta's eldest daughter, is kind enough even to send them a congratulatory card, wishing the couple well. Luigi and his family not being present for a significant event in Angela's life is nothing new. Although she feels their absence, her wedding day is one of the best days of her life.

It takes every cent the young couple has saved to pay for their wedding. On their wedding night, George and Angela are counting the money from their gift envelopes, holding their breath to see if they have enough cash to finish paying for the honeymoon. They will fly out to begin their honeymoon in Bermuda first thing in the morning and have given the resort only a deposit. The couple sighs in relief when they count just enough money from their gift envelopes to finish paying for the honeymoon. When George and Angela return from their honeymoon, they have only $20.00 and a thirteen-year-old car to their names, but it does not even frighten them. The newlyweds are living in the furnished, three-room apartment that Angela and her sister had shared. Teresa had moved out of state a few months before the wedding. Angela works as a receptionist and office clerk, and George is an apprentice. With both salaries, they make just enough money to subsist. But their poverty does not matter to them. They are so in love and so happy that nothing else matters except being together.

After two years of marriage, George and Angela want a child. They give up after two more years of infertility treatments and stop going. But around their fifth wedding anniversary, Angela conceives their son. The couple joins the first-ever birthing class for parents the hospital has established, and George will take part in his wife's labor and delivery. Nine months later, on their way to the hospital to deliver their child, Angela takes George's hand.

"For the rest of our lives, it will never be just us two."

Her husband squeezes her hand.

The couple experiences a miracle when their perfect son, Alexander, is born. George thinks his son's birth is the most fantastic thing he has ever seen. Angela cradles Alexander in her arms, and his existence moves her so much, she cries. Her son is her miracle baby, and she cannot believe he is hers, created through love, and a gift from God. Angela vows to be the absolute best mother possible. The new mother does not want her precious son to share her with anyone. So, Angela decides, with George's agreement, not to have any other children. Angela wants to devote her time and energy only to Alexander, showering him with the love and attention she never received as a child. No child is loved more than Alexander Limoges. She thanks God for him every day.

Two days after Alexander's birth, it amazes George when they go to the hospital nursery, and Angela identifies their son only by his feet. The hooded tops of the newborns' bassinets are against the viewing glass, so neither their faces nor name tags are visible. When the couple requests their son and the nurse lifts Alexander, sure enough, he is the baby whose feet Angela has identified.

When they were planning their family, George and Angela decided they wanted to raise their child with Angela being a stay-at-home mother. To make their plan a reality, George works two jobs after Alexander is born. Being with her baby full time are among the best years of her life, and she loves every minute she spends with her son. It amazes Angela how blessed she is.

The impulsive and emotional decision to prohibit her father from attending her wedding is among the greatest regrets of Angela's life. Several weeks after their marriage, George informs his wife that Luigi was standing in front of the drugstore across the street from the church on her wedding day, watching from afar. Angela never spotted her father. When she finds out, her heart breaks for him. Luigi's daughter thinks she is the worst person on earth.

How could I have been so cruel? Angela is still ashamed to this day when she thinks of how hurt her father must have been, and she has wept many times at the thought of the pain she caused him.

They soon reconcile, but her father's neglect of her and selfishness never changes. For one year, Sophia and her husband rent the second-floor flat in the two-story house that Angela and George own. Luigi comes to visit Sophia and her beautiful toddler daughter often. He passes Angela's first-floor door coming and going, and never once knocks to say hello.

To George's chagrin, Angela cries every time. Alas, she is still waiting for Luigi to show his love for her.

At long last, Angela realizes her dream of attending college when Alex is four years old. George continues working two jobs so Angela can both attend school and be home with Alex. Her university has a preschool program for the children of their adult students. Angela takes her classes in the morning while Alexander attends the nursery school, which he loves, and they go home together at noon. The schedule is perfect. Angela even becomes the President on the board of directors at the nursery school.

While George works his second job in the evening and Alex is sleeping, Angela does her schoolwork. On weekends, while Angela studies, writes papers, and prepares for exams, George tends to Alex. Once their son is in elementary school, Angela works as a full-time research assistant at a local psychiatric hospital while receiving her education.

Angela graduated from college *summa cum laude* with a perfect 4.0 GPA. With George's blessing, she attended law school on a full scholarship, doing teaching assistantships in return. George has always been so generous with Angela, doing whatever necessary to help her meet her goals, and he is a gift to her. He always encourages Angela to reach her potential, and he is secure enough in himself that whatever she achieves does not threaten him. No one was prouder than George on the day Angela received her Doctor of Jurisprudence degree. Although Angela drove herself to excel and worked hard, she could never have done it, or not so well, without George's help, encouragement, and support. It was a team effort.

After Angela finished school, George opened and grew his own business. Angela tried to be as supportive of his career as he was of hers. As well, Angela was building her law career and was committed to helping children. When Angela joined a law practice where they carried many custody cases, the firm assigned several of them to her. She loved the work and was successful, winning every case.

Once Alex went to college, Angela opened her law firm handling only child-custody cases. She dedicated herself to her law practice, doing a percentage of *pro bono* work for single mothers without means to pay. At retirement, Angela's firm had a widespread, sterling reputation and was very prosperous. One of the most challenging decisions she ever made was letting go of her life's work and active control of her company.

* * *

Alex and his wife, Sarah, have two children, and both Angela and George adore their grandsons. They are the joy of their lives, and they are a close-knit family. Being retired enables Angela and George to attend the boys' sporting and school events, and the added time with her grandchildren makes Angela's retirement rewarding. Now she has settled into her new, less demanding life, Angela plans to volunteer, doing something to help children.

As an adult and before reprocessing her childhood, Angela learned new and surprising information about her family of origin from research and conversations with her older siblings. Her maternal grandfather did not die before her birth. Her grandparents had divorced (a scandalous rarity in the 1920s), and her grandfather was alive during her entire childhood. He had been living in Indiana and created a new life for himself as if Angela's grandmother and their children never existed. Angela now wonders if he ever missed her mother (who was his first child) or thought of the grandchildren he never met.

Her mother had a brother, but Angela and the rest of her siblings never met him either. The uncle had lived in Indiana, too, which leads Angela to think he had stayed with his father after his parents divorced.

Did they divide their children as possessions? If so, how heartbreaking!

One piece of information plagues adult Angela: The reason her half-siblings moved out of their home after their mother's death. Decades after the older children left, Angela learned they moved out because Luigi was cruel and abusive to them, which horrified and sickened her. He beat the boys without mercy, often causing bleeding and welts when the belt he wielded tore into their flesh. Angela was unaware it was happening and had no memory of arguments or shouting in the house. Teresa, who had been old enough to remember the abuse, disclosed it to her sister.

"We were lucky we didn't stay together in that house because it was like living in hell."

"What do you mean? What else happened?"

"Things went on that I can't discuss. You're better off not knowing; believe me."

Angela did not press Teresa to tell her, but now, having revisited her childhood and putting the pieces together, she can guess what happened. If she is correct, it did not involve Luigi. When she heard of the physical abuse her siblings suffered at the hands of Luigi, the information helped her understand why her half-brothers and sisters feared him when they were young, and why they always hated him.

Angela gets tearful when she realizes Teresa and the older siblings have had to live with such memories. There is no excuse for Luigi's abuse of his step-children. While he could not undo the damage, Angela hopes her father regretted the violence and showed remorse. She shudders to think of the emotional damage done to his victims.

As she struggled to forgive Luigi for the person he was, she reminds herself that people change. Her father mellowed with age. Whenever he got angry, he swore in Italian, and his anger subsided in no time. Once, Angela repeated the Italian phrases she had heard her father spew in anger so many times before, and he got upset with her.

"What does it mean?"

"Never mind. Don't ever repeat those words."

Angela remembers the exact phrases, but she finds it too embarrassing to ask anyone fluent in Italian to translate them. They might have been in dialect versus classic Italian, had incorrect spelling, or were too awful because even Google Translate did not convert the phrases to English for her!

Conversations with her older siblings provided Angela with information that humanizes her mother in her eyes. Besides her fourteen living children, Viola had two deceased children. Angela thinks such loss is more grief than any mother should have to bear. An older sister said their mother reported that each time she cradled one of her new infants in her arms, she remembered the children she lost. Viola did not believe she could survive the loss of her first child. Her sweet, handsome boy died of polio two months before his fourth birthday. Viola was only twenty-two years old, and she described the pain as unbearable. The older sister said having to take care of her other child, Millie, helped their mother get through those long, dark days of unspeakable grief. Recently, Angela saw an old photo of her young mother holding her firstborn on her lap. The picture reflected Viola's love for her son as she gazed at him. Her eyes beamed with adoration.

Then, the mother's first child with Luigi, who was a boy too, died a short while after birth. His given name was his father's nickname, Lou, and his middle name, Panama, was in honor of Luigi's favorite place in the world. He had visited Panama when he was in the U.S. Army and fell in love with the country. Luigi vowed to return there one day. Angela imagines the pain of losing his first child, his namesake, must have scarred Luigi. To Angela's knowledge, her father never once mentioned his first son to any of his other children.

Despite this added information, Angela still has many unanswered questions. Her parents living together without being married was so unconventional during that era, and Angela could not find any record of divorce for Viola or her husband.

Could it be that my parents never married because my mother never divorced her first husband? If so, why?

As for the Carcieri siblings, Teresa, Anna, and Margie are in close relationship with Angela. Teresa lives much further away, so they don't see each other often, but they speak on the phone, and their hearts are irrevocably intertwined. Anna hosts most of the major holidays, and Angela is attached to Anna's five children, especially Sophia, but she loves every niece, nephew, grandniece and grandnephew whom she knows. Sweet Katherine has many physical problems and stays at home, so Angela does not see her much. They talk sometimes, and Angela loves Katherine and her three delightful children. Gino and Donald estranged themselves from the family decades ago. Angela accepts that, too, and does not want it to be any different, but she wishes them well.

In adulthood, Angela had casual relationships with her older siblings, Robbie, Evie, and Laurie, but their visits were infrequent. She has born no resentment toward any of her half-siblings for leaving them. After her mother's death, she never again saw the brother who moved to Alaska, nor the oldest sister, Millie, after the one chance meeting at the beach when she was a child. Mary only visited her sisters one time after the brief visit they had when Angela was around eleven years old and living with the Kowalskis. Approximately twenty years later at a family reunion cook-out Anna planned and hosted, Mary showed up and stayed for only an hour. Laurie, too, was absent from Angela's life for around two decades.

Angela's half-siblings have passed now, except for Laurie, who has disengaged from the family. This past Christmas was the first time in two decades, Angela did not receive a

Christmas card from Laurie. Her sister has not answered the several calls Angela made, she has no voicemail or email, and has not responded to the note Angela wrote her, requesting Laurie telephone her. Laurie's decision saddens Angela, but she accepts it without bitterness, knowing Laurie might have issues to resolve.

Angela knows God has been with her every step of the way. The blessings she has received are countless, and she loves her life. She was victorious over her challenging childhood and beat the odds by becoming a successful professional and living a joyful, productive life. God is ever faithful.

13

THE HEALING PROCESS

Angela healed and found the peace she was seeking. She got the professional help she needed to healthily face her fears, accept the pain, and reprocess her childhood. The fear she carried for so many years no longer exists. Through reviewing her life as a foster child, Angela gained insights and made conclusions that gave her a different perspective and enabled her to let go of old resentments.

For Angela, an essential part of the healing process was the ability to forgive. Although she had a natural capacity to do so, forgiving lifelong resentments required more than she had. Her faith was the source of that extra ability.

As a child, Angela believed she belonged to God. The child had always thought Jesus's death saved her by making it possible to go to heaven, but it was not assured. Her entrance depended upon her behavior. As an adult, Angela came to understand there was nothing she could do to earn her way to heaven. She could never be good enough or deserving enough. Angela now knows that Jesus's death assures her salvation—a gift, free to those who accept Him as their Savior.

This acceptance does not mean Angela never has problems or struggles. But being sure of her eternal life and final destination helps her get through those struggles with the confidence that she is never alone and will prevail. Angela reasons that because God forgives her for every sin, both past and present, then she should forgive others.

Luigi was who he was, his daughter realizes. He could only be himself, nothing more and nothing less. Wanting and hoping for him to be different was futile and a waste of precious time. The man she spent a significant portion of her life waiting for did not exist. Angela now knows if her expectations of Luigi had matched the reality of who he was, she would have spared herself much disappointment and many tears. She has learned to appreciate and remember the good things about her father, which were many, and forgive the flaws.

In attempting to heal from old wounds, Angela tried to reassess her childhood with more wisdom and objectivity than she had as a child. So she tried to see things from the perspective of the people she resented by putting herself in their shoes. In doing so, Angela could recognize the many disappointments Luigi must have had in his life. As mentioned earlier, he was the black sheep of his family. He must have felt the disapproval, and even though his family's feeling toward him were because of his behavior and choices, it did not eliminate the pain. Given his respect for and devotion to his parents and siblings, their disapproval must have hurt. And that was only one of his many disappointments.

Yes, Luigi's refusal to give his children a chance for a better life by prohibiting their adoption was selfish. Good families asked to adopt Donald and Katherine, but Luigi did not sacrifice his desires for the welfare of his children. But Angela can imagine how difficult giving up a child is. Luigi did not have the strength. The man's selfishness was his most glaring flaw. The children lost their mother, and Luigi lost his wife. On the heels of such a tragedy, it had to be painful even to consider losing his children, too. Angela is not sure she was ever strong enough to have given up her child, and she can sympathize with Luigi's position.

Only now can Angela imagine how difficult it was for her father to give custody of his children to the state. While it resolved his immediate problem, it must have broken the man's heart to give up his "little rabbits," as he referred to them. Luigi said he planned for the state's custody of his children to be temporary, and he always kept his parental rights. During childhood, Angela thought Luigi wanted to give his children away, and she resented him. Now she understands, under the circumstances, her father saw no choice.

In reviewing his life, Angela realizes Luigi never returned to the country of his dreams. She wishes she surprised her father with a trip to Panama before he died. Over thirty years have passed since his death, and his daughter regrets not telling Luigi how much she loved him. Angela wonders why we only realize such things too late to make corrections.

While not excusing Luigi for everything or condoning his behavior, Angela has forgiven him for how he treated her. She cannot overlook the pain he caused others or the abuse of her siblings—nor is it her place to forgive those things. Luigi made it easy to find fault with him, but he possessed many good qualities, too, and Angela wants to present a balanced picture of him. Luigi never abandoned his children as many single fathers do. Although poor, he always worked hard and paid child support to the state for the care of his seven children. Their father visited them and kept them a part of his life. Though his contact with his children lacked compared to what they needed, it was to Luigi's capacity.

Further, Luigi gave his children many lovely memories of times together at the beach, park, and his apartment. The children always enjoyed their time with him. Angela has cherished memories of holiday traditions with Luigi, his fantastic Italian food, and playing after-dinner card games as a family. She admired her father's respect for and devotion to his parents and siblings. Luigi loved his children and grandchildren to his ability. Angela is glad her father stayed a part of her life and forgave her for her cruelty to him. As a mother, she is grateful Alexander got to enjoy his "Gramps." Angela loved Luigi, can now accept their relationship and cherishes his memory. She misses him. A tremendous burden on her heart has lifted.

Too, Angela can now view her mother with more compassion. She struggled with anger towards Viola after learning of Luigi's physical abuse of her older siblings. Angela wondered how and why Viola tolerated Luigi's brutal assaults on her children and accepted the other horrors to which Teresa alluded. Those questions plagued her, but she did not know Viola well enough to answer them. Angela remembers her mother as a strong, kind, and nurturing woman, but those characteristics are inconsistent with someone who accepted such abuse. Her mother's real character mystifies Angela, but she reminds herself that human beings are never that simple. Nobody is all good or only bad. When we are not in their position, we find it easy to judge others.

In attempting to understand Viola, Angela imagines what life was like for her. The woman had fourteen children to raise and no job. She was still grieving the loss of two children, Luigi's family did not accept her, and Viola's father and brother estranged from her. Other than her children, her only family was an elderly mother in Michigan. Thus, Viola had nobody to turn to for help and had minimal options. After considering everything, Angela decided her mother did her best with what she had.

It baffles Angela why Luigi's family did not come together to aid him and his children. With two active parents and seven adult siblings (with six spouses), his family was large enough to help. Luigi's youngest sister tried. She took Angela and her three younger siblings to her apartment for lunch one Saturday afternoon before the state gained custody. The youngest, Angela's three-month-old brother, Donald, preoccupied their aunt. As an adult, Angela heard the same aunt (who was childless) wanted to adopt Donald. When Luigi refused, the aunt ended her involvement and never visited the children after that one afternoon. If she could adopt the baby Angela reasons, she could have helped Luigi (and the baby) by taking care of Donald instead of allowing him to go into foster care. Angela resented her Carcieri relatives for many years.

Since reprocessing her childhood, Angela has released her long-standing resentments toward her relatives by taking a different perspective. Before reviewing her childhood, she only focused on the Carcieri family's failure to help her father or his children. Angela never considered that they, too, had their own families and sets of problems. She heard nothing of their struggles, but Angela is sure, as humans, they had them. Plus, taking full responsibility for the care of a child is no small undertaking, and they might have had financial constraints.

While Angela still thinks her relatives should have done more (e.g., at least visit the children), she realizes resentment changes nothing and no one, except the person harboring the bitterness. Resentment blocked her from being her happiest and interfered with her living her best life. She has been able to release the resentment and is better for it.

Sometimes, we cannot and should not forgive. One instance is if the offense is against someone else. An example is Luigi's abuse of his stepchildren. Angela does not have the right to forgive Luigi for what he did to someone else. Only the abused can forgive the abuser. Another condition that makes it impossible to forgive is the lack of remorse. Angela's rape is an example of this. Because she cannot know whether Ted was remorseful, forgiving him is impossible. Repentance is necessary for absolution.

But Angela can now see the assault for what it was and recognize it can no longer hurt her if she refuses to give it any power. The rape was a tragedy, doing significant damage to Angela. She was not aware she allowed it to continue to hurt her. Her psychologist helped her see she had a choice and taught her how to leave it in the past. By reprocessing the rape in therapy, she removed its power to hurt her any more. In trying to bury it and pretend it never happened, it continued to haunt her. The therapy work helped Angela to release it and lay it to rest. The reprocessing stopped the nightmares.

Angela's foster parents, even the negligent ones, played a vital role in her life. Angela is grateful to them. They took strangers into their homes and sheltered them. Angela cannot imagine what might have happened to her otherwise. To her, even a deficient placement is better than homelessness or living in an institution. Several of her temporary caregivers were decent people who provided proper care, which was a blessing. None were better than the Wilsons, who will own a piece of her heart forever.

14

ALL'S WELL THAT ENDS WELL

March 15, 2019
5:00 p.m.

Seventy-one-year-old Angela has just rushed home with the fresh ingredients for her usual Friday night, make-your-own-pizza family dinner. Her son, Alexander, and his family will arrive in an hour. Ever since they installed the brick pizza oven on the back patio a year ago, these dinners are a tradition the family looks forward to each week.

The Limoges so enjoy living in a warm climate year-round now. Angela is more than grateful for Alex and Sarah's decision to move to the same location right along with them when she retired. The pizza dough has been proofing for a few days, has excellent elasticity, and is ready to go, but Angela still must slice the pepperoni, grate the cheeses, chop the veggie toppings, and prepare the salad.

Ralph, their handsome and spoiled black lab, is underfoot and wanting his share of the food he sees and smells. Angela gives him a chunk of fresh mozzarella, which he inhales and licks his chops, lusting after more. Her two grandsons, eleven-year-old Aidan, and fifteen-year-old Noah have bottomless pits for stomachs, so their Nonna Angela has more than enough food.

The clock in the hall chimes six, just as Alex, Sarah and the boys burst through the door full of smiles, chatter, and energy, getting Ralph excited. They are on time for a change, surprising Angela.

"Hi Nonna," Aidan, says. Noah, who is already towering over Angela, is right on Aidan's heels, and they both give their grandmother a big hug.

"Hi, guys! I've been looking forward to seeing you all day." Angela squeezes her beloved boys.

"Hi, Mom. Is it ready? I'm starving." Alex kisses Angela on the cheek, then hugs George.

"So am I." Sarah gives more hugs as she greets her in-laws. "I didn't have any lunch today."

Too impatient and hungry, everyone munches on the pepperoni, cheese, and other toppings. The blazing hot pizza oven only takes a few minutes to char and blister the crust to a perfect Neapolitan style, and, in no time, they have had their fill of the delicious pizza and salad. Angela does not know where slender Noah puts so much food!

"Nonna, you make the best pizza!"

"Why thank you, Aidan. That's because I have the best pizza-eaters for grandsons." Both boys hug her again.

"Love you, Nonna."

"Love you, more." Angela is floating on air.

After everyone clears the table, they break out the playing cards and two cribbage boards, as is their custom. Alex and Sarah play head-to-head on one board, while Nonna and Papa, along with their grandsons, play a partners' game on the other board. They play a double-elimination tournament, in which the winners on each board then play a single head-to-head round, as do the losers. The final two winners go head-to-head for the championship title, bragging rights, and an extra scoop of ice cream. To decide partners in the tournament and who will deal first, they each cut the deck. When George cuts the lowest card to win the deal, he brags of his prowess in the game, and the boys laugh.

"Papa, do you always beat Nonna when you two play?" Noah smiles, knowing how his grandfather will respond.

"Of course!" George looks directly at Angela with a smirk on his face.

"Yeah, in his dreams." The competitive Angela is not letting him get away with that fib.

"Well, that's because she cheats," George teases.

The boys chuckle as they egg on their grandparents. Angela looks around the table at the beautiful, smiling faces of the people she loves most. This family is her greatest success. Angela realizes she has come full circle. By sitting around the table and playing cards after dinner, they are reenacting what her family did at Luigi's house when she was a child. Making that association causes her to smile. Nonna Angela hopes that Aidan and Noah's memories of these times will be as sweet as hers.

My family, right here in front of me, is the family I longed for my entire childhood. This family, these bonds, and so much love and happiness are what George and I have built together. Alex and his sons are not only gifts to us but are our legacy to the world. No one could be more blessed than I.

"Nonna, it's your turn." Aidan is too excited to wait.

"Three." Angela starts the round by putting the three of hearts on the table.

"Ten." Aidan plays a seven.

"Seventeen for two." Noah smiles as he matches Aidan's seven and pegs two points.

"Twenty-four for six." George is gloating as he plays the third seven and pegs six points. He and his partner, Aidan, celebrate by slapping hands in a high-five.

"Thirty-one for two, plus twelve for fourteen!" Angela slaps the unbelievable fourth seven onto the table and pegs fourteen points, oozing glee from every pore while her partner, Noah, cheers and her sweet Ralph barks in excitement.

APPENDIX A

Seven Steps
To Heal Old Emotional Wounds

While writing Angela's story, the author, Dr. Sandra Duclos, uncovered, illuminated, and defined the seven steps Angela used in the process of healing old emotional wounds. She shares the seven steps with you for informational purposes. Please be aware: healing old wounds does not mean you erase your memory or have no emotion when you remember the hurts. Breaking free means the old wounds no longer haunt you or interfere in your life.

WARNING:

I offer these steps for informational purposes only. The actual reprocessing is more complex than this cursory list. This list is not a replacement for psychiatric care. This seven-step process might require professional help, depending upon your mental status and the seriousness of the wound. Do not do this on your own if:

1. the event was severe or traumatic, such as a rape, a physical attack, or a life-threatening event;

2. you are under psychiatric care or are taking psychotropic medication;

3. you have Post-Traumatic Stress Disorder or severe psychiatric symptoms, such as flashbacks, depression, or suicidal thoughts;

4. you feel overwhelmed in attempting this process.

If any of the above apply, get help from a mental health professional, as Angela did. Further, take as much time as you need. Stop whenever you need to; do not overwhelm yourself. You can always take a break and return to the reprocessing later or stop the process altogether.

USE THESE STEPS ONLY FOR NON-TRAUMATIC EVENTS

1. **Facing the pain.** Face your fear and the emotional pain you might encounter head-on, and recognize fear only has the power you allow it. Suffering is a natural part of life. Stop avoiding it. When we avoid emotional distress because of fear, we empower it. When we accept the pain, our anxiety decreases, and we weaken fear's power. Remember: the offense is in the past. It can no longer hurt you.

2. **Reprocessing.** This step entails revisiting the offending incident and reviewing it in as much detail as possible, engaging all your senses.

3. **Understanding.** Depending upon the event, try to gain a greater understanding of what, how, and why. Examine the offending incident with more objectivity than you did when it happened, using your adult mind versus the mind of a child. If they meet the conditions for forgiveness (see Chapter 13), try to take the perceived offender's perspective. We often see and understand things we would not otherwise. Try to put yourself in their shoes.

4. **Acceptance.** Accept what happened as reality. You cannot change it and pretending it did not happen does not make it go away. Do not mistake acceptance for approval. When we see an event for what it was, we can use that knowledge to have our expectations match the reality of the situation. Angela's unrealistic expectations of Luigi caused her repeated disappointment and pain. See the offender for who they are versus who you want them to be. Look at the facts, not the spin you have put on them.

5. **Forgiveness.** When it is possible and makes sense, forgiveness is freeing. When we hang onto resentments, it hurts only us, not the offender. Not all is forgivable (as mentioned earlier, in Chapter 13), and that is okay. If it is unforgivable, don't allow it any power over you. Banish it from your life after accepting it for what it was. It cannot continue to hurt you if you release it.

6. **Release.** When we can accept and forgive, letting go follows, especially when we understand how holding on keeps us stuck and in pain. If you cannot forgive, you can still release. It has already hurt you too much; do not allow it to continue. Take power over it by releasing it: banishing it from your consciousness and refusing to allow it to affect you any further.

7. **Gratitude.** No, we should not be grateful for being hurt. But, as Angela did, we can learn from our bad experiences and use those lessons to improve our lives. Whether the pain has strengthened us, or we are less gullible, or more determined, we have gained something we did not have before the incident. Let's be grateful for what we learned, not for the offense itself. Be thankful we are free of it, and that it ceases to have power over us.

APPENDIX B

Insights by Dr. Duclos

As challenging as Angela's childhood was sometimes, it was a cakewalk compared to the daily nightmare some children live. Every experience, both positive and negative, made Angela who she is today. Pain is as much a part of life as joy, and we can learn and grow from it. We need it if we are to be fully human. Angela's need to be in survival mode gave her the ability to read people well, which helped in her career. Hardship often breeds character. Angela is stronger, more driven, and more determined because of her childhood. She knows how to delay gratification and can adjust to most situations. Angela can withstand difficulty, and it does not cause her to fall apart or run away, but to endure and seek solutions.

I am not claiming abuse, neglect, or treating children as if they are deficient or unworthy are positive, nor should we ever tolerate them. However, we can turn bad situations around for good. Those rough experiences in Angela's life pushed her to excel, to prove those who thought less of her because she was a state ward were wrong, and she was as worthwhile as anyone else. Her need to prove herself benefitted her by being the driving force, pushing her to excel, and it contributed to her success.

Because she endured deprivation, Angela is aware and appreciative of her blessings; she takes nothing for granted. Gratitude enriches her life and feeds her happiness. Her challenging childhood also made her self-motivated. While growing up, Angela learned she had to rely on herself. No one else would fix things or make them better for her. That realization motivated her to work hard and achieve.

As a child, Angela hoped and prayed for Luigi to show up, bring her family back home, and show his love for her. When that did not happen, she hoped and prayed for a loving home and family to bring her happiness. She counted on the old proverbial truth "All things come to those who wait." Now, she realizes a greater truth: the only one she was waiting for was herself—we are the only ones who can make ourselves happy. It must come from within us. Although Angela had help along the way from many people, she was self-motivated and the driving force behind her success and happiness.

Happiness is a choice; it is not luck or good fortune. For Angela, it is a by-product of many things: being in a relationship with God, gratitude, hard work, faith in herself, maintaining hope despite the odds, making sacrifices, loving and helping others, and the way she perceives things, regardless of her circumstances. We can focus on the negative, be miserable, and get stuck in the problem, or we can focus on the positive, be appreciative, and search for solutions. Even if we feel we are all alone in the world, we can find happiness and enrich our lives by reaching out to help others.

People who do not learn these lessons often turn to drugs or alcohol to escape or manage difficult situations or overwhelming emotions. If we do not believe we have the power to change our circumstances, all we can do is try to escape them. Angela never even tried drugs and was drunk only once in her life when George was with her, and she knew he would make sure she was okay. She abstained not because she was or is more virtuous or stronger than anyone else, but because being in command of yourself is crucial in survival situations. One of Angela's greatest fears was not having control. It was way too precarious for her. She learned early in life that when you are not in control of yourself, negative things happen. Now, she is more able to let go of her need to control everything. While difficult for her, she is improving—a work in progress.

Angela says she could go on about all her weaknesses, flaws, and the lingering insecurities, too, to which those who know her well can attest. But despite her flaws, I hope her story will inspire others, regardless of their circumstances, to endure, push forward, hope, and know they can succeed. If we use a lousy childhood, bad luck, or any other excuse, it only keeps us stuck and wallowing in self-pity. We can break free and improve our lives and the lives of others. The power lives within us to choose happiness and success, and the key is in the way we think. We are in control of our thoughts and can change them.

APPENDIX C

Recommendations for Improving Foster Care

The foster care system is essential and has saved many lives. Angela is grateful it was there when she needed it. It beats living on the streets. However, the mechanism is flawed, at least in the state where she spent her childhood. Social workers face the burden of such massive caseloads they cannot tend to all the children in their care. When Angela was in foster care, her caseworkers had up to fifty children assigned to them. With so many to attend to, they can do nothing more than put out fires. Although there has been a slight improvement since then, bulging caseloads is still a significant problem.

Because Angela was a well-behaved child, she rarely saw a social worker, and they never got to know her or her needs, Sometimes, she did not even know her social worker's name. Continuity of care was nonexistent. Had her social worker had the time to build a relationship with her, Angela might have revealed what was going on in the Schneider and Lundgren homes. Perhaps it could have prevented her rape.

The lack of continuity regarding social workers has several causes, including frequent turnover of employees, low pay, insufficient funding, and not enough caregivers. For the 2018 fiscal year where Angela was in foster care, the state earmarked only 2.26% of the entire state budget for DCYF for all expenses, and the amount of those funds specified for child welfare was only 1.77% of the total state budget. For the same fiscal year, the transportation budget was two and one-half times what it was for DCYF, and over three times what went to child welfare. More funding to increase state social worker salaries and hire more workers to lower caseloads will help with continuity of caseworkers for foster children.

Until and unless we make children a priority by adequately funding the agencies responsible for their care, it is unlikely we will see significant positive changes. Investment in our youth will pay dividends in the long run. It will be much less expensive for the citizens to fund better care for our foster children than to pay for prison cells, mental health institutions, joblessness, drug addiction, and homelessness when these children become adults if they do not receive proper care as children.

We also need policy changes as much as increased funding. When Angela and George decided they wanted to help by becoming foster parents, they went through a DCYF training program. Back then, as now, DCYF considered foster care short-term placement. They told the potential parents at the training sessions not to get attached to the children they would care for, and they discouraged bonding. Their practice was to move a child if she or the foster parent was getting too attached because the goal was reunification with the biological parents. Also, the foster parent had almost no input into DCYF decisions. If a child is being sent to stay with an abusive parent for the weekend, the foster parent must comply. Today, the goal is still reunification, and foster parents still have no say in the decisions the state makes regarding the children in their care.

Angela and George did not even consider taking a child into their home without loving that child as if he were their biological child. They refused to consider handing a child in their care over to an abusive adult. Therefore, they dropped out of the program. While they recognized the children needed help, they could not be part of a system that does not put the children's best interests first.

As Dr. Duclos sees it, the most significant problem in both the court system and DCYF is the automatic goal of reunification. While it sounds noble, in reality, it hurts the children. An automatic goal of returning children to their biological parents is not always best for them. Parental rights seem to take precedence over child rights. Yes, people make mistakes and can rehabilitate themselves and improve, but how many chances should they get when a child's life is at stake? While the parent is in and out of rehabilitation programs, for example, and given repeated chances and more time to get their act together, the child languishes in a flawed system. Also, a significant number of foster children who reunite with their parents return to foster care, some of them multiple times.

Why not impose time limits on the parents and limit the number of chances they receive? The parent should know about the policies up front, which might provide them with an incentive to better themselves. They might love their children, but love is not enough. Love does not make you a fit parent, and parental love should not supersede the child's best interests.

Angela and her siblings were in foster care for almost their entire childhoods. She was in six different placements between the ages of five and sixteen. Her father's rights as a parent superseded her welfare. He was not abusive, nor drug-addicted, nor mentally unstable, but either he could not or would not take custody of his children to provide them with a permanent home. The state should have given him a timeline with a concrete plan for reclaiming custody of his children. DCYF could do periodic checks with him to determine progress and even provide temporary financial aid to make reunification possible.

We pay for foster homes, including placements in homes of relatives (which is an improvement since Angela was in foster care), why not subsidize needy families to enable fit parents to keep their children at home? If a parent is unable or unwilling to meet the goals and deadlines set for them, then they lose their parental rights, and the children become adoptable. If the children's age makes them unadoptable, then they could live in permanent foster homes. Stability and consistency of placement are crucial for a child's sense of well-being.

* * *

In the state where Angela grew up, the policy is to give parents one year to get themselves on track and reclaim their children, which, in theory, is a good policy. However, there are no hard and fast rules. They determine a disposition on a case-by-case basis. When the one-year deadline expires, it is not uncommon for the parent to get an additional year (e.g., the mother gets one year to resolve her drug problem, then develops depression and receives another year, even though the drug problem is still active). Then what? How long does the child have to suffer because we are more concerned about the parents' rights than the child's?

Another pressing issue for foster children is safety. As mentioned earlier, Angela was in some neglectful homes and some abusive ones. She rarely saw a social worker, and no adult was checking on her. While a license is an essential step in ensuring minimum foster parent qualifications, it does not guarantee the placement is as fit as it may have been when the people were approved. Therefore, DCYF should re-inspect the licensed foster homes regularly for cleanliness, adequate food, and such. Social workers should build relationships with the children in their care, and do regular visits with their charges, looking for signs of abuse or neglect, such as poor hygiene, being underweight, having bruises, showing symptoms of depression or severe anxiety. They should also talk with the children about their care. When we listen to children, they often reveal a lot of information.

A recent news broadcast reported the death of a young girl with special needs in an unfit foster home after allegedly being left in a bathtub of water for eight hours. Several people (teachers, neighbors, caseworkers) voiced concerns about neglect to DCYF, but they did not investigate the placement and accusations until after the child's death.

In Angela's childhood state, they have a shortage of temporary homes. DCYF's solution was to adopt an initiative to increase the rates they pay the foster parents and make the licensing process quicker and easier. While I have no issue with higher compensation for these caregivers, I believe that hurrying them through the licensing process is the opposite of what should be happening. More training of the prospective caretakers (e.g., classes in child development and positive behavior management) and more evaluation of their fitness, including psychological assessment, might be a better solution.

In addition, we could provide more resources for caretakers to help the children and themselves. For example, they can have access to professional counseling to help them deal with the children, their own emotions, or burn-out. Even offering regular group meetings for foster parents with a professional facilitator might help them feel less isolated and normalize what they are experiencing. These suggestions would make for better temporary or long-term stays, so the state wards would have more continuity of placement and be safer in those homes.

Another issue I would like to address pertains to changing a child's placement. First, children should have closure and an opportunity to process their feelings about leaving their current home. Such processing might prevent them from blaming themselves or thinking they are unlovable or as disposable as an old pair of shoes. In non-emergent situations, a one-day notice to leave a placement is inadequate. We might also introduce the children to their caretakers and let them see their prospective home before living there. Would not any adult want that for themselves? Who would move into a new home without ever seeing it or take on a roommate they never met? I would not. Many of us have had a potential babysitter meet and interact with our child before engaging the person to babysit. Isn't it even more critical to do the same before a child lives with the person? Most times, there is no choice where the child will live, but the children still deserve the respect of being listened to and shown their thoughts and feelings matter, even if there is no choice.

When these children move to a new placement, carrying their meager belongings in trash bags only feeds their belief that we also consider them trash. We should find a way (for example, seeking donations) to supply or loan inexpensive suitcases, duffle bags, or backpacks to children for moving their possessions. Angela thinks this might be a way for her to help make improvements.

Finally, forcing Angela to exit the system at 16 years old was appalling. At least, that has improved. In the state where she grew up, a child ages out of the state's custody at 18 years. A proposal is now on the table to increase that age to 21 years. We are wrong when we force a minor child to exit the system before finishing high school. By doing so, we increase the likelihood they will drop out of school to work full time to support themselves. A child's chances for success decrease if they leave the system before graduating high school.

Foster children have three times higher high school drop-out rates than children from other low-income families[1], with only 20% of those graduating high school attending college as compared to 60% for other high school graduates[2]. Fewer than 2% of foster children complete a bachelor's degree before the age of 25, whereas 24% of the general population do[3]. If a child quits school, we should offer them occupational training.

All children should receive advance notice before their release from the system. We should offer classes to prepare them for independent living, career counseling, information about college and educational grants and loans. Their social workers, or even volunteers, can help facilitate the process and ensure that they have a place to live and a means to survive. Yes, some foster care policies have changed since Angela was a state ward, but many problems remain, and many states still have broken systems. Our children deserve better, and so do we.

Foster children are in the state's custody through no fault of their own. Their status is not equivalent to a juvenile delinquent or a criminal. They are not inherently bad nor destined to live worthless lives. Like anyone else, if we prejudge them without evidence, we will probably be mistaken. Like any of our children, they have feelings, intellect, hopes, and dreams. They need love and can give love. They can aspire to and achieve great things and be productive members of society.

When we make our children a priority by sufficiently funding the agencies responsible for their care and changing inadequate policy, we give them a shot at a happy life. Well-cared-for children are more likely to become well-adjusted, contributing adults. When we invest in them financially, emotionally, and intellectually, we invest in our future.

ENDNOTES

1. www.nfyi.org/issues/education. 2016
2. www.pewtrusts.org/en/,,,/for-foster-care-kids-college-degree s-are-elusive. Dec. 7, 2017.
3. foster-care-newsletter.com/foster-youth-graduate-at-low-rates. Mar.1, 2018.

ABOUT THE AUTHOR

Dr. Sandra Duclos is a recently retired clinical psychologist who spent more than twenty-five years in private practice. During her career, she helped countless people overcome a broad spectrum of problems and empowered them to be masters of their fate. She has published professional papers on her original research related to the self-control of emotional experience.

Although retired, Sandra's purpose and passion are to continue helping others to live their best lives through writing, coaching, and teaching. She and her husband, Ferman, live in Rhode Island where they raised their adult son and now enjoy their two amazing grandchildren.

Connect at **DrSandraDuclos.com**

YOU HAVE READ THE BOOK,
NOW TAKE YOUR NEXT STEP

*
**

CAN YOU IMAGINE AUTHOR DR. SANDRA
DUCLOS COACHING YOU ON A JOURNEY THAT
LEADS TO A MORE JOYFUL LIFE?

*
**

CAN YOU IMAGINE RELEASING YOUR OLD
EMOTIONAL WOUNDS AND RESENTMENTS,
FREEING YOURSELF TO LIVE YOUR BEST LIFE?

*
**

CAN YOU IMAGINE LEARNING HOW TO CHOOSE
YOUR OWN EMOTIONAL EXPERIENCE AND
CHOOSING HAPPINESS

*
**

TO LEARN MORE, CONNECT AT
DrSandraDuclos.com

Made in the USA
Middletown, DE
01 November 2019